Broken in Boston

for Chris

Published by Mindstir Media, LLC
1931 Woodbury Ave. #182 | Portsmouth, New Hampshire 03801 | USA
1.800.767.0531 | www.mindstirmedia.com

Printed in the United States of America
ISBN-13: 978-0-9983183-2-5
Library of Congress Control Number: 2016918019

Broken in Boston

By Rick Shakalis

MINDSTIR MEDIA

Chapter One

Change and Hope

"Hey, you big creep! Keep your mitts to yourself!" Hope Davis protested sharply as she shoved her date's uninvited hands away, ending his clumsy attempt at foreplay. "If you're this frisky maybe you should talk to your wife about it."

A startled Frank Barnes recoiled, reacting to these words like he mistakenly touched a live electric wire, "How did ...?"

"I thought I saw a tan line on your finger and figured it might be from a wedding ring. Now I know for sure, take me home."

This much anticipated date had quickly deteriorated into one where each person wanted to be anywhere but in each other's presence. These things tend to happen on blind dates when both parties discover the person they are with is not even close to the one they had been led to believe they were.

Frank gathered himself for a minute, reluctantly starting up the Knox Limousine he had borrowed from the lot and pulled on to Beacon Street for the return trip to Jamaica Plain, mission unaccomplished. This limo, while apparently failing to impress his female companion, would be described as a "real lady killer" and "a hotel room on wheels" tomorrow to his more appreciative prospective male customers.

People on the street stopped in their tracks to peer inside its windows, thinking they would see a ball player or starlet up close, an exciting celebrity encounter they could brag to their friends about.

What they did see was a stylishly dressed man, sporting a straw boater, behind the wheel, accompanied by young woman with Hollywood star looks who they didn't recognize. The most remarkable thing about the man and woman was not who they were, but how miserable they both looked. How anyone lucky enough to be in this impressive automobile, obviously having the world by the tail, could still be remotely unhappy was beyond their comprehension.

Frank glumly maneuvered over the sometimes bumpy roads wondering if he was starting to lose his touch. Showing up in this eye-catching car, dressed in the latest fashion, taking a hit of whiskey from his lucky flask in the glove box and parking at his favorite secluded spot next to the Public Gardens, this date was supposed to be a sure thing. At least that was what his business partner, Al Piquette, had lead him to believe.

Piquette was manning the floor a couple of weeks ago when Hope showed up, selling her a top end Atlas Model H with very little effort, laughing under his breath, "Frank would kill to be in my shoes. That girl's a regular Florence Lawrence! It looks like he picked the wrong day to take off."

Noting how unusual it was for a woman to buy an automobile without a man being present, he casually asked about the whereabouts of Mr. Davis, and Hope simply said, "There is no Mr. Davis." This piqued Al's curiosity to the point where he called on an acquaintance working for the Boston Police Department "to learn Hope Davis' story" and maybe figure a way to use her circumstance to his advantage.

∞

Frank and Al had built one of the most successful business ventures in the growing city of Boston based on selling automobiles. The two men had been friends for a long time, working at various sales jobs, when Al hit upon an idea that he was convinced could make them both rich. If they pooled all their resources and opened a car dealership that carried not just one, but many types and brands, they could hit the big time.

That was back in the year 1905 and the automobile industry was still in its infancy, with many small shops manufacturing a wide variety of automobiles, all vying for market share. In Massachusetts alone between 1861 and 1930 there were over 180 such companies that produced all sorts of cars: steam powered cars, ones that ran on gasoline or kerosene, even, surprisingly, a number that were electric, capable of traveling up to a hundred miles before needing a charge. American ingenuity was in full swing.

The two erstwhile entrepreneurs, with a mechanic friend tagging along, called on one of these fledgling companies and offered pennies on the dollar for one of their hand-built, well-engineered automobiles. The cash starved business reluctantly accepted, a few luxury extras were added, and the car was promptly resold for big bucks. They repeated the process until they acquired enough inventory to open a lot on Boylston Street, which soon expanded, and their dealership became a going concern.

Frank particularly liked all his cars to be "fully loaded", which, appropriately, also was an apt description of him half the time.

Both men started raking in the cash, which not only made them suddenly visible to the city's elite, it also helped cover up some of their bad habits. For Al, his Achilles heel was his penchant for gambling, making the part of his nature that allowed him take an entrepreneurial chance to open this business in the first place to also put him in hot water on a regular basis. He was into the bookies all over town and had to keep the cash flow up just to keep his knees intact.

Many would consider Frank's behavior as a tireless womanizer to be his bad habit, but for him, it was just a harmless "hobby". Although he had a wife and two daughters, he saw no reason to change his ways because he always managed to be discreet and his family was well taken care of financially. He was pretty sure his wife didn't know about his secret life, and even if she did, he was about to buy the family a new home in Brookline, one big enough so there should be no complaining about his frequent "late nights at work."

∞

It was now the year 1910 and with their car business thriving, Frank and Al were in their early thirties and living life to the fullest. It wasn't such a bad idea considering the average life span for a male in Boston at this time was 52.

"So Frank, do you realize this is your lucky day?" Al addressed his partner when he showed up at the showroom, putting down his *Racing Form* a week before the ill-fated date. The floor was packed with all manner and brands of automobiles they had acquired: four Shawmut Touring Cars, six Morse Torpedoes, two Stanley Steamers, a Stevens-Duryea Big Six, five Metz Roadsters and four Bailey Phaeton Electrics to name a few. All examples of exemplary engineering, or at least hopefully built well enough to last before their limited warrantees ran out.

Al had a habit of leaning back in his leather swivel chair with his arms folded, prominently displaying the *Carpe Diem* sign on his desk. Like Frank, Al was a sharp dresser, 'Dress for success' was another one of their mottos.

Frank knew full well that Al would probably be inducted into 'The Bull Shitter's Hall of Fame' on the first ballot someday, but because Al was capable of coming up with a great idea from time to time, he was open to at least listening to his pitch.

"There's this drop dead gorgeous young woman who bought the top end Atlas H off the floor yesterday whose name and number I have in my pocket that wants to meet you, Frank. Not only is she a knockout, I heard she is easy. In fact, she might be the first woman I met that wants it as bad as you. You won't even have to spring for dinner."

Frank hadn't been too busy with the ladies lately and his ears perked up. "Sounds too good to be true, like one of our cars," Frank grunted, quietly.

"No, no, I know how you love the ladies, Frank. I wouldn't kid you about something like this," Al answered, dripping with sincerity.

"So, Al, what's the catch?" Frank asked suspiciously, knowing there was always a catch.

"No catch, Frank," Al answered, feigning a hurt intonation. "I just thought I could help you out with your dry spell. But now that you mentioned it, if I give you this young lady's number, maybe it could square up that bet I owe you."

Ah, the catch, Frank thought as Al successfully engaged Frank's familiar battle between his brain and his ever-restless loins. It wasn't really any sort of a contest, the usual side declared a very quick and decisive victory.

"Okay, but she better be a looker."

∞

This "date of a lifetime" which Al had set up was quickly becoming apparent to be based on false pretenses to both parties. Hope, as advertised, indeed was far more than pretty, but in no way was she "easy", at least not with Frank she wasn't.

Hope was led to believe Frank was, "A true gentleman, a man you could have a future with." Another dead end was more like it, making the difficult decision she had been mulling over easier.

At this point of the date, driving back to Jamaica Plain in tense silence, Frank figured he had nothing to lose, so why not try another tactic? Sometimes you think the sale is dead and take a stab at one more pitch and, *wham*, the next thing you know you're filling out paperwork.

"Miss Davis, I think we got off on the wrong foot, let's start over," Frank said in his best soothing sales tone, hoping to keep his pursuit of this striking young woman in play.

"Maybe we could come to some sort of arrangement that could work out for the both of us."

"Arrangement? What am I, some sort of a business deal to you? Is this your idea of treating a girl right? Just take me home, you jerk," an exasperated Hope said, upset with this world champion horse's ass from that well populated stable of clueless Clydesdales she always seemed to end up with.

Frank and Hope, silently sitting next to each other, traveling in the darkness over the streets of Boston, Massachusetts on July 14, 1910, had seemingly nothing in common. But, as the fates would have it, this was simply not the case. Major changes were about to happen in both of their lives within the next year, for one by circumstance, the other by choice.

Frank never realized the same relentless capitalistic system that was making the United States an economic powerhouse, the one that gave him the opportunity to strike out and build a lucrative business, could also take it away. The United States was becoming a highly competitive country and if you were lucky enough to be successful, you had better stay on your toes.

While the two automobile tycoons were enjoying their newfound wealth and status, they were so distracted by their "hobbies" they never paid attention to Henry Ford's revolutionary idea of making quality automobiles on an assembly line, and thus affordable for everyone. Ford's idea was a game changer, selling 10,000 Model T's in 1910 alone, and he was just getting started.

Frank and Al were like a couple of dinosaurs, happily stomping around in the primordial ooze, blissfully unaware of "the big one" about to hit.

Another major change was about to blindside Frank. It concerned his marriage and two children, which he put just enough time and energy into to place him in the "Family Man" category to the casual observer. Unbeknownst to him, his totally fed-up wife had already made plans to dump the philandering Frank, a bold move that he never thought she had the courage to pull off.

Frank thought he was careful to always cover his tracks, successfully fooling a lot of people, but he didn't realize you can never fool the laundress.

Significant changes were about to happen in Hope's life as well, starting with a life-altering decision that she had been wrestling with for some time, not at all happy with herself and the direction her life was heading. Despite being blessed with remarkable, head-turning beauty that made her coveted by men and women alike, she felt broken inside.

She was twenty-two, and ready to become the woman she wanted to be, not the one everyone saw her as.

∞

Hope's father had drifted off with another woman leaving her as a two-year-old, her mother Delores, and four-year-old sister Ellen to their own devices in a world dominated by men in the late 1800's. Single women trying to support a family had few choices back then and Delores felt her best option was to entertain "gentleman callers".

Hope had hazy recollections of her childhood, but one incident made quite an impression on her. When Hope was about four, a distraught woman came to the door with a child in her arms and when Delores answered it, the woman started screaming at her mother, punctuated with the word 'whore' many times. When the confrontation ended with a slammed door, Hope asked her mother what that word meant and Delores brushed it off saying, "Oh, that's just what a woman calls another woman when she is jealous of her looks."

The parade of men through the household continued unabated.

The majority of these "uncles" were habitual drunks, pitching in with a few dollars here and there, usually found sitting at the kitchen table with Delores sharing her ever present bottle of whiskey, knowing as long as she could provide a bottle she wouldn't have to be alone. Hope always sought their attention and looked for approval from these men even though they were far more interested in that liquid in their glass than her. Most were harmless, but then there was David Van Trap, who brought more than whisky with him into the household.

∞

The United States had a major problem with opium, heroin and cocaine in the 1800s and by 1890, the country had more addicts percentagewise than any other time in its history, including today, and far more per capita than any other country. The use of these drugs was so common America was called "a dope fiend's paradise", an unfortunate result of the confluence of three main factors.

First, a quirk found in the Constitution charged individual states, not the federal government, with the responsibility of controlling drugs. Without universal strong laws to monitor dangerously addictive substances, drugs were able to flow freely from state to state with little consequence. This oversight was not properly addressed until 1914 when Congress passed The Harrison Act, finally criminalizing the non-medical use of opium and its derivatives such as heroin, as well as cocaine. Unfortunately, by then these drugs, and the misery associated with them, had spread to every segment of society.

Another factor was the medical community, including no less than the U.S. Army Surgeon General who enthusiastically endorsed opium, and then morphine, to patients for a variety of ailments in the 1800s. Mistakenly thinking morphine was a non-addictive version of opium, it was also prescribed as a treatment for alcohol addiction, a practice that would continue for decades. In 1884, the esteemed Sigmund Freud published an article in a prominent medical journal praising cocaine as "a magical drug" and, he, too, listed it in the category as "non-addictive". The United States was awash with drugs; doctors had no qualms about giving them liberally to their patients, and some of the doctors, too, had become addicts.

The third major cause fueling America's drug problem was the lack of requirements to list ingredients of over-the-counter medications. The majority of these "patent medicines", elixirs and tonics, easily obtained at the local apothecary, contained opium, heroin and/ or cocaine. They were sold to an unsuspecting public to treat such ailments as depression, menstrual cramps, toothaches, and "to soothe and calm children". Many people took these drugs regularly without even knowing it, becoming accidentally addicted. Women in particular fell victim, partly due to the extravagant advertising of these opiate patent medicines guaranteed to relieve "female troubles". Even a new popular beverage introduced in 1886, called *Coca-Cola*, was laced with cocaine. It would not be until 1906, when laws were passed to require companies to list ingredients on consumer products, that the public was shocked to learn they were ingesting additive drugs and began to reject them.

In 1910 drug addiction finally began to slowly decline, but because these drugs were so easily available for such a long period of time, they had become firmly entrenched in American society. There were still a large number of addicts in the United States at this time, as there would be going forward. Duncan Troupe was one of them.

∞

He was a child of privilege, and although his record at Boston Latin High was mediocre at best, Duncan's father used the classic combination of connections and alumni donations to secure his underachieving son a place at Harvard as long as he tried out for the football team. Duncan was a big, strong kid and played running back his senior year at Latin and showed some promise.

The Harvard coach saw otherwise. When his quarterback was knocked down in a scrimmage, Duncan never helped him up, just turned his back and walked back to the huddle, making him look selfish and a poor teammate in the eyes of the coaching staff and team veterans.

Duncan would be given a chance to prove himself by head coach Doug Crook, to see if he was more than just another spoiled rich kid on an ego trip, by having his star linebacker laying a lick on Troupe, "ringing his bell", to see what he was made of. That one hit was enough for Duncan to develop a severe case of "fumble-itis", become disinterested, and led him to be cut from the team. Troupe hated football ever since.

Never missing a party, but far too many classes, Duncan was able fake his way through the rehash that is freshman year. But by sophomore year when the real work began, his poor habits put him on the academic watch list and he was in danger of being sent home, prompting him to hatch a plan.

There was an overachieving Irish kid from a humble background on his floor, who Duncan was sure he could convince to take a couple of tests writing "Duncan Troupe" at the top of the page. Duncan was surprised when the kid turned down the money, and shocked when he turned him in to the dean, who immediately kicked the disgraced Troupe out.

Fredrick Troupe, humiliated by his son's behavior, made a deal with the school to keep everything discreet and promptly shut Duncan off, attempting to teach his spoiled son a lesson.

Duncan, furious and unrepentant, blamed his father, Harvard and especially his ungrateful Irish dorm mate for not knowing his place and how the game is supposed to be played. Troupe then scraped together any money he could get his hands on and left home, and began going by the name of David Van Trap after shaving his head and growing a beard.

Feeling down and wanting to be numb, Van Trap started with heavy use of liquor, smoked his share of opium, dabbled with all manner of drugs until he discovered heroin, which magically seemed to make his troubles disappear.

Within a year of being an ivy-leaguer, Duncan Troupe, alias David Van Trap, became a true "junkie", a name coined for people like him that frequented junk yards, picking up scrap metal to sell in order to support their habit.

Van Trap met Delores Davis at Kelly's bar when she was in between men, and, becoming less and less picky as each man left the scene, invited him home. He noticed there was no other male in the household, and without a sheriff in town, knew he was free to "be himself".

Van Trap liked Delores just fine, but the minute he laid eyes on Hope, he was like a man possessed, and given his addictive personality, would stop at nothing to have her. Hope had developed into an attractive young woman, still somewhat naïve and, miraculously up until now, relatively unaffected by her dysfunctional surroundings. She always craved a man's attention, which the frequently present David was only too happy to provide.

He managed to be alone with Hope as much as possible, showering her with dime store trinkets and compliments, manipulating her as only a true addict could. When he felt the time was right, he introduced her to his best friend, the dark hearted prince, heroin.

The next six months were a blur for Hope, a muddled time she could never fully remember or explain. Van Trap managed to get her hooked on heroin and she soon became as dependent on it, and him, as a person could be. Her whole world revolved around her next fix as her physical appearance began to change, her eyes becoming sunken and her normally clear skin appearing blotchy.

One hazy week ran into the next, until one day, everything changed: Hope discovered she was pregnant. Realizing her drug use could do harm to her baby and without anyone's intervention, she defied the odds and managed to stop using heroin.

Her eyes, no longer glazed over, began to see Van Trap as the predator he really was, and without a partner to share drugs with and feeling harshly judged by the three Davis females, he silently slithered away.

Hope considered herself lucky to even be alive. She was free of Van Trap and drugs, but now alone with a daughter, Emily, to support, she needed to survive on a different level: she needed money. Hope, no longer naïve, decided to use her physical beauty to her advantage by seducing the richest man she could find, offering to act as his mistress, while taking him for as much as she possibly could. Men had used her for as long as she could remember and now it was time for her to return the favor.

She gained employment at a bustling shoe manufacturing plant on Bickford Street in Jamaica Plain, affording her to keep a small apartment for herself and Emily, but she had much bigger aspirations. Asking around, she learned the owner of the factory was one of the wealthiest men in Massachusetts and had apparently dallied with some of his female employees, making him the perfect foil.

Hope coyly set the trap and he walked right into it, a seduction Cleopatra herself would have approved.

Except her well thought out, cynical plan didn't quite turn out as expected. How could a typical arrangement for sexual favors in exchange for creature comforts transform into a relationship in which Hope developed genuine feelings of affection? It was a turn of events that surprised and confused her, adding another layer of conflict to her already complicated life.

Like Hope, her lover had left formal schooling in the 8th grade, not unusual as only 6% of the population graduated high school at this time. But, unlike others, he never stopped learning, reading everything he could get his hands on, even after he became highly successful. Once he discovered Hope never properly learned how to read he arranged a tutor for her, and much to everyone's surprise, discovered she was extremely bright. She became an avid reader herself. Reading opened a whole new world to her.

It was when she read a particular book, *The Story of My Life* by Helen Keller, that Hope took an honest accounting of her life and the root cause her underlying rage and frustration. When Helen Keller wrote of "being locked in a silent prison of her own body" as a result of being born deaf and blind and how her anger subsided when she miraculously learned how to communicate, it felt like these words in the book were written just for Hope.

If Helen Keller could change her life, why can't I? Hope asked herself. She felt like she was also locked in a prison, paradoxically from the curse of being born beautiful, which had caused far more grief in her life than joy. Until this empowering lover came into her life she had come to the conclusion all men just wanted to use her for their own pleasure, as if they were playing some sort of game she didn't fully understand and she was worth more points to them based on her looks.

Maybe if I were born plain, men would have left me alone and I wouldn't have a child at home to support.

Hope had dreamed their affair could lead to a future together, but he decided to end it when his personal and professional lives became totally unmanageable. On that last confusing morning they spent together she offhandedly mentioned she was "late", but wasn't completely sure if he heard her.

When they parted he gave Hope a large amount of cash, which at first offended her, but now she was grateful knowing he did this to help put her life back together, to get a fresh start.

Hope always used the ruse of being a widow explaining away Emily, but now with the arrival of baby Tommy, she began to hear whispers of 'whore' from members of so-called polite Boston society behind her back. Being called that word cut her to the quick, like a long, cold dagger to her heart, especially when she found out the true meaning of the word, not her mother's version.

Boston was settled by Puritans, a humorless, judgmental lot that if you study history, you would agree, made the Taliban look like a warm, fraternal order by comparison. Despite its recent influx of immigrants that helped to neutralize such self-righteous, pejorative ways of thinking, the 'City on the Hill' still clung to Puritanical values.

Boston was not a good place for a single woman to raise two children out of wedlock, at least in the early 1900s it certainly wasn't.

Hope had already seen a lot of life at a young age and knew this much to be true: It was a man's world; they held the power and any woman that didn't have one in her life was at a severe disadvantage. Unless she could marry, her children surely would end up being the subject of prejudice and have a difficult life.

The way things stood it would be next to impossible to attract a suitable husband unless she made a major change.

Hope was convinced there was only one path for her to take: the best way to save herself and both her children was to give one of her children away.

∞

As the handsome Knox limousine rumbled into Jamaica Plain, Frank Barnes broke the awkward silence as they approached Hope's sister's neighborhood, making a last ditch sales pitch.

"What's wrong with me? I've heard you're not that picky, why not me?" now whining.

"You've heard what about me? You don't know anything about me! Just let me out here."

Frank grudgingly pulled the limo over to the curb. Leaning over, his vest straining against his newly acquired sign of wealth, he opened Hope's door. His parting gift was the pleasure of his scent: a mix of witch hazel and Jack Daniel's No. 7.

"You know, Hope, maybe we…"

Hope pushed the door open and just as quickly slammed it before having to endure another minute in the presence of the type of man she no longer had use for in her life.

The strident *Click, Click, Click* of high heels pounding the sidewalk announced to anyone within earshot that Hope was in no mood to be approached, especially by any creature that happened to be male. When she reached home, her sister was on the couch quietly reading from the stack of magazines on the coffee table, and Emily and Tommy were fast asleep upstairs.

"You're home early, this must be a record. What happened?" Ellen, Hope's sister and best friend asked, already forming an opinion on how the evening had most likely unfolded given her early return.

"You came on too strong again, didn't you? I know you can't help it."

Hope collapsed on the couch and gave her sister a quizzical look.

"What are you talking about, Ellen?"

"Well, I just read an article in *The Lady's Home Journal* that talks about your problem. You should read it."

"My problem? Now, what would that be?"

"I think you might be one of those nym-pho-maniacs they talk about."

"What? You think I'm a maniac?"

"Not just a regular maniac, a *nympho*-maniac. It's a woman that wants sex all the time and can never say no, especially if she has had a drink or a 'reefer'. It's just not me saying this, it's scientifically proven and they wouldn't print it if it wasn't true."

"Well, I said 'No' tonight, that's why I'm home so early. You and your magazines, I'm no 'nympho', whatever you call it. Let's face it, we're both a little mixed up when it comes to men."

Ellen just listened for a full twenty minutes, admiring her sister for at least trying to have a relationship with a man, unlike her, who up until now had dated very little. Men generally scared her.

They talked the better part of an hour and the conversation got animated when Ellen eventually offered,

"Maybe you should contact Tommy's father and let him know he has a son. See if he will give you some of his money, which, if you believe what you read in the papers, he has plenty of. If he doesn't bite, we can threaten to contact the papers and shake him down."

"No!!! Absolutely not!! He was the one man that treated me right and I don't want to complicate his life, he has enough on his plate."

"Okay Miss High and Mighty, don't pop an eyelet on your corset. That was pretty much your original plan, after all."

Hope sat quietly for several minutes before finally proclaiming,

"There's only one way to fix the mess my life is in. I am going to put Tommy up for adoption into a stable home, just like we tried before, using that agency. Tommy is younger and a male; it has to be Tommy. With just Emily maybe I can meet a decent man to settle down with and make a real family."

"Hope, are you absolutely sure you want to go through with it this time? Remember how you almost went through with the same thing, and then changed your mind at the last minute? What makes me think you won't do that again?"

"It's true, I thought I could raise two children with no father at home, but this last year has been hell for both me and them. No, this is our only way out."

"I hate to bring this up but that adoption agency we went to only deals with children up to three years old."

"That's right, I forgot. Now we will have to deal with some second-rate agency, I guess. So much for that plan," Hope said, now deflated after expending so much energy on her introspective conversation.

Ellen answered immediately, obviously already having given her sister's situation a lot of thought.

"Last year we had Plan A, this year we need to go to Plan B."

"Plan B? What's Plan B?"

"Put another pot of coffee on and I'll tell you."

Chapter Two

Gone To Boston

Over ten percent of the population of The United States claims Irish heritage, making the story of how so many arrived here one every American should know. When I asked a prominent Irish-American his take on the Potato Famine he told me, "Well, that was a long time ago and we Irish don't like looking back on it, things are so much better now. But, on the other hand, there are a lot of lessons to be learned there..."

Warning: If you are squeamish or English you might want to skip this chapter.

Boston has been traditionally associated with foods such as baked beans and cod, but none actually had a bigger impact on its history than potatoes, specifically Irish potatoes. When the Irish Potato Famine began in 1845 the population of Ireland was eight million, but by 1852 it had developed into a disaster of such magnitude it caused over one million deaths in Ireland, roughly the same number of Americans that died from all the battles of WWI and WWII combined. It also caused nearly two million Irish citizens to emigrate to other countries, dispersing around the globe, with the largest percentage landing in the port city of Boston.

It has been said natural events can destroy crops leading to food shortages, but it is government policies that turn troubling food shortages into deadly famine. The natural cause of the Irish Potato Famine was *Phytophthora infestans,* a fungus that causes late blight, capable of turning a heathy potato plant into a stinking pile of mush practically overnight. This blight hit all of Europe starting in 1844, but only in Ireland did people die from starvation by the hundreds of thousands. Why only there? Well, if the Irish Potato Famine were a crime scene, the English government had its fingerprints all over it.

For centuries England had developed a rigid social structure, and at the top of this class-based pyramid stood a select few individuals born of royal blood who carefully guarded their lineage. Alongside the royals sharing power in The House of Lords were high-ranking members of the Anglican Church, both entities receiving the benefits of tax collection without the burden of paying taxes themselves. While representing only 2% of the population, this powerful alliance of church and state held the lion's share of the land, most of the wealth, and kept strict control over the citizenry.

One rung below on the social class ladder were the landed gentry, including such coveted titles as squires, lords, barons, baronets and knights. The landed gentry were able to obtain fabulous wealth through land holdings and were given the elevated status of "gentleman" if they could demonstrate that they obtained this money passively without the indignity of work.

This sought after class could maintain an opulent lifestyle, including impressive estates with a full complement of servants, if their political connections granted them large enough tracts of land and they could manage to squeeze out as much profit as possible.

To maintain the extravagant lifestyles of those in power it required a constant source of vast amounts of money. England, under the banner of God and King, began to spread its tentacles around the world enveloping weaker countries, unabashedly extracting revenue from them often by unsavory means such as forms of slavery and exploitive working conditions. Citizens of these captured countries were often portrayed in the press in such racist terms as "aborigines and sub-human", implying that they were somehow worthy of their fate.

Taught from a young age to believe the Anglican Church was the one true religion, many Englishmen felt anointed as the chosen ones in the eyes of God. Between feeling innately superior due to their race and with God squarely behind them, some of the English ruling class developed personality traits of a person deriving their self-worth from acquiring wealth and power without a trace of empathy or remorse, even if their methods were unethical, immoral or illegal.

England had conquered Ireland, a poor country consisting mostly of farmers, on and off for some eight hundred years before deciding how this fertile country could best be of service to The Crown: Ireland would become the breadbasket for the expanding British Empire.

Large parcels of Irish land were doled out to members of England's landed gentry who quickly gobbled them up, choosing to control their newfound prized source of income as absentee landlords.

Irish country farmers no longer owned the land that had been in their families for generations, having been reduced to little more than landless serfs. Whenever they tried to resist, their powerful occupiers crushed them on every occasion.

England continued to slowly, methodically ratchet down its control of the Irish people. Landowners learned they could make the most profit on their holdings by either subdividing their newly acquired acreage and collecting as many rents as possible, or push the Irish off their property altogether to create pasture land for cattle.

Now, in order to make the rent on a now much smaller piece of land, Irish farmers had to devote a bigger percentage of their farm to grow crops to export, leaving just a small plot to feed themselves and their families. The ones that had been thrown off their land had no choice but to retreat to higher, rockier and much less fertile ground.

The Irish were methodically being squeezed into a box by their English landlords, a box that eventually would take the shape of a coffin.

Potatoes, which had always been a staple of the Irish diet, now took on a much more significant role. The variety grown was dubbed "The Irish Lumper", not a particularly attractive potato with its rough, bumpy skin, but extremely nutritious, packed with vitamins and minerals. Because it had enough nutritional value to sustain life, grew well in even poor soil, and took up very little space, it became the life-sustaining crop for farmers and their families.

All the while, as the Irish's lot in life was becoming more and more difficult, the propaganda machine in England was at work. *Punch*, a satirical magazine, regularly depicted "Paddy" as a simian wearing a top coat, eating only potatoes and getting into drunken brawls plotting murder, especially against the English working man. Tales of farmers huddled in huts while practicing mysterious Catholic rites in caves caught the rapt attention of fearful English schoolchildren.

If such talk seemed repugnant to some Englishmen, who could they complain to? The Anglican Church, the moral authority of the British Empire? Hardly, they were in on it.

As horrible as life in Ireland had become, for some it was about to get far worse. In 1649, an organization named The Irish Confederate

Catholics had gained political support in Drogheda and Wexford in a quest to regain land rights back from the English. This disrespect to the Crown by these ingrates needed to be attended to.

Oliver Cromwell, a radical religious zealot, was dispatched to quell the insurrection armed with "moral authority from God" and used this pretext to go far beyond his mission. Once the rebellious Irish were quickly dispatched, he ordered his soldiers to slaughter as many Roman Catholics as possible because, according to him, "Catholics were inferior, putting faith in Papal authority over strict interpretation of the Bible." It was Cromwell's version of ethnic cleansing, and he was merciless.

Once the carnage finally ended, he divided up large parcels of former Catholic land, colonized some of it with Protestant Scots, and deeded the rest of it to his soldiers as reward for their meritorious service.

Even some of the English eventually thought his actions were egregious. Cromwell viciously massacred so many innocent Catholic men, women and priests, historians have charged him, and rightly so, with genocide. Years later, in some bizarre fit of conscience, his fellow Englishmen took full measure of his actions, exhumed his body, and hung the bastard posthumously.

Laws were enacted to further persecute and marginalize Catholics. They could no longer: vote, hold public office, work in civil service, own a weapon, own property worth more than five pounds, be educated in or outside of Ireland, practice their religion, all while being required to pay a tithe to the Anglican Church.

But, the new edicts weren't all bad. If Catholics converted to the Anglican Church, they would be given back their full land rights.

For a country as beautiful as Ireland was to look at, it was becoming an increasingly uglier place to live in. The best and brightest young people left, escaped more like it, looking for work "across the water" in England, or for a lucky few, America.

By 1840, the industrial revolution was in full swing and England was in the fortunate position as the first country to fully embrace it. Having harnessed the power of steam, blessed with an abundant coal supply, a ready source of capital and an educated workforce, they were quickly becoming "the workshop of the world" and a more affluent middle class was growing. English citizens also had the added benefit of cheap food available to them, no small part due to Ireland, and with more disposable income they were able to purchase manufactured goods that made their lives more comfortable.

Contrast that to Ireland, trapped in a sort of bizarre time warp, the world passing it by. The Irish were a repressed people barely surviving on small plots of land without a chance of participating in the new world economy. In 1840, as the standard of living in England was ascending rapidly, the fortunes of Ireland were headed in the opposite direction. Irish citizens were so played out, a census taken that year documented that half the population still lived in mud huts.

It would take a cataclysmic event such as an invasion to finally break the stranglehold Britain held over the Irish people. An invasion would occur, not from an invading army brandishing state of the art weaponry, but from one of nature's humblest single-celled organisms.

In 1845, when tiny spores of *Phytophthora infestans* latched onto droplets of water from fog enveloping the Irish countryside, it drew little notice at first. When a few potato plants started to wither and potatoes became black, foul smelling and rotten, confounded farmers consulted village elders well versed in traditional crop management but they, too, were no help. No one had seen anything quite like this before.

Things got progressively worse. Over the next year, blight insidiously spread into every county, and with their primary source of food rotting in front of their eyes, the Irish began to go hungry.

People, living on a farm that produced food that was still being exported, were going hungry.

Word reached London of Irish starting to die of starvation due to a potato blight, and, as if Irish luck weren't bad enough, Sir Charles Trevelyan happened to be the English government official in charge of dealing with the problem. Much like Cromwell before him, he had a strong evangelical upbringing, showed no empathy or remorse for his actions and made no attempt to hide his disdain for the Irish. Instead of recognizing it as a tragedy of human suffering, he embraced The Great Famine as "the judgment of God" upon the Irish providing an "effective mechanism for reducing surplus population".

Common sense would dictate to aid the Irish all Trevelyan had to do was temporarily stop the exporting of food until the famine subsided, but that is not what he proposed. Envisioning Ireland as a perfect place and this the perfect time to introduce strict capitalistic principles, he constructed a series of workhouses where "people could earn money for food instead of being dependent on handouts." Weak, starving, desperate people were charged with building roads that started nowhere and ended nowhere, getting paid eight cents a day to buy food.

All the while food exports continued unabated, often at gunpoint.

By 1846 in Ireland, when more potato plants got sick and died, so did the people. Severe malnutrition led to cholera and dysentery and the deaths began to add up. The most vulnerable were the first to die, the older citizens, and horrifyingly, the children. So many dead and dying Irish children and babies, yet Trevelyan remained unmoved, resolute.

The Irish were not the only ones dying. So were the English landlords, dying in a different way, of embarrassment, worrying estates and hunting lodges in their family for generations might be lost under their watch due to this current "unfortunate set of circumstances". Tenants, no longer healthy enough to farm and pay their rent, were evicted in large numbers by ruthless landlords seeing their privileged life slipping away.

The scene that was repeated over and over went something like this: Local Irish police surrounded the cottage and threw the tenants out, backed by the local British constabulary. The home was then pummeled by battering rams, and what was left was often burned to the ground.

Like a scene from a sci-fi horror movie depicting the walking dead, starving people roamed the countryside, including hollow-eyed mothers clinging to dead babies. Searching for any morsel that could sustain life, they scrounged for anything they could get their hands on including the green grass of the Emerald Isle itself.

Only when all hope was lost they entered the workhouse, a virtual petri dish of disease, a dismal place they considered life's final indignity.

Hundreds more died, then thousands, then hundreds of thousands. By 1847 even the English had enough and chartered ships allowing the Irish to emigrate, principally to the United States and Canada.

The United States was transforming from a mostly agricultural economy to one based on manufacturing and newly built factories clamored for more workers. The United States government signed on to take in 1 million Irish immigrants, the most of any country, and Boston being the closest city to Ireland, took in thousands.

To say when the Irish landed in Boston they were welcomed with a city-sponsored Saint Patrick's Day parade held in their honor could not be further from the truth.

In the 1840s, the population of the proper city of Boston was 115,000, and was run by "Brahmins", Anglo Saxon Protestants that traced their lineage back to the Mayflower. When 37,000 bedraggled, mostly Catholic Irish survivors dressed in rags showed up, the locals were horrified, feeling invaded due to their sheer numbers.

Many Bostonians that had generously donated to the Famine Relief Fund were fine with the concept as long as the Irish stayed in Ireland, but when they started showing up on their doorstep, they turned their backs on them as well.

The Irish, used to living on farms in the countryside colored in vivid shades of green, were directed to the North End and its tightly packed brick buildings and cobblestone streets, their world now a bleak study in browns and grays.

With more and more destitute Irish pouring into the North End, it soon became so overcrowded it began to resemble a shantytown, looking far more like Calcutta than pristine Beacon Hill. Feeling the familiar sting of prejudice, they kept to themselves, forming a close knit community, and took any unskilled jobs available to them when not faced with "Irish Need Not Apply".

Uneducated, with few work skills and still vilified for their religion, the Irish found themselves placed at the bottom of the scrum of other immigrants scrambling for survival in their new, fast-paced, competitive country.

It was as if the Irish race had been shattered into a thousand pieces over a period of generations, and here they were, broken in Boston. Many felt they weren't much better off here than they were in Ireland, but time would prove otherwise.

The Irish, what was left of them, had made it to the United States, a country envisioned by its founding fathers not to be a guarantee that it would fix you, but instead be a country that guaranteed you an opportunity to fix yourself. No matter who you were or where you came from, at least you had a chance to claw your way up the economic mountain and make a better life if you wanted it badly enough.

The Irish had a rough start, to be sure, far worse than most other immigrants coming to Boston, but they had a huge advantage over others: they had numbers on their side. There were so many Irish Catholics now living in Boston, a marginalized Massachusetts Democratic Party took note and began to court this large voting block hoping to make inroads into what until now was the most Republican state of them all.

For over eight hundred years of English rule the Irish were held powerless, relegated to no more than peasants, and all they had to show for it was living in mud huts and surviving on lowly potatoes.

Some thirty years after the large influx of Irish immigrants arrived from The Great Famine, after discovering the power of the ballot box and organizing Democratic political machines in every ward and precinct, Hugh O'Brien, Boston's first Irish Catholic mayor was elected in 1885.

The Irish had one of their own in the most influential position in Boston and finally began to feel that intoxicating rush of power.

And they were just getting started.

Chapter Three
The Mary Magdalen Adoption Agency

The Brahmins and others in positions of power that enjoyed the good life that America had to offer, and not wanting to share it with any newcomers, formed the "Know-Nothing" movement, an anti-Catholic, anti-immigrant third political party. The upstart party played on the fears of the citizenry and was so successful in Massachusetts it swept nearly every political office in 1854, including Governor. This xenophobic splinter group fortunately was short lived, declared unconstitutional, disbanded, and became no more than an ugly footnote in Massachusetts history.

Once the "Know-Nothing" hysteria subsided, the Catholic Church was free to increase its presence in Boston, starting with an ambitious program of building churches followed by bringing in its storied institutions such as hospitals and parochial schools.

Rowdy Irish kids capable of taking on any tough urchin on the street soon found themselves no match for nuns wielding rosary beads in one hand and a ruler in the other. In short order these rough and tumble Irish kids got "cleaned up, straightened up and taught up" by the good sisters, finally giving them the ability to apply for more skilled, better paying jobs.

The Church also constructed a number of orphanages, and if there ever was one on Boston's Tremont Street in 1911, it just might be called The Mary Magdalen Adoption Agency.

Regarded by everyone in town to be Boston's finest, it discreetly handled the delicate life altering matters of adoption without being judgmental of the unwed mothers despite its potentially pejorative name, Mary Magdalen being the arch-type "fallen woman" in the eyes of the Catholic Church.

The agency was tirelessly run by The Sisters of Jesus the Merciful, a Catholic order of nuns that traditionally served God by tending to the indigent, sick, mentally challenged and other forgotten souls of society. The order decided to expand their mission by taking over a failed adoption agency on Tremont Street and within a year had it running in peak efficiency. By all measures, business was booming.

Renovations on the newly acquired property, which took up much of the budget, consisted of raising the ceiling height. The official word was to allow for more air circulation making it healthier for the babies, but others thought it was a subliminal way to intimidate the clients looking to adopt, drawing on that old trick, making people feel small in similarly designed spaces such as churches and courthouses.

The dedicated sisters always fulfilled their duties wherever the order sent them, but working at The Mary Magdalen Adoption Agency was considered a plum assignment. Like most women everywhere, they loved being around babies.

The Mother Superior in charge was Sister Apollonia, quite a tall woman possessing an unusual amount of energy that could be off-putting, even intimidating, when you first met her. When dressed in full habit, wearing her order's distinctive, gravity defying white starched Cornett head covering, it gave her the appearance of an intimidating avenging angel. Women in her presence generally kept quiet and respectful; men, however, had a much different reaction: she scared the hell out of them.

Hope had an appointment with the intention of putting Tommy up for adoption with the agency more than a year ago, but had what could best be described as a panic attack and left in the middle of the interview. The whole incident was stressful and embarrassing for Hope, but she still was able to observe and ask enough questions to figure out the agency's system of record keeping. Now, although she was well aware Tommy was too old and did not qualify for adoption, she had set up another meeting. When ushered into Sister Apollonia's office, Hope was relieved to see all the furnishings were situated the same as her last visit.

"Good morning, Miss Davis, I remember you from before. I apologize again for the way our interview ended, did you have another child?" asked Sister Apollonia, her flowing habit resembling a judge's robes, the stark contrast between the black and white of her clothing representing guilty or innocent, evil and good. With all the people she was in touch with she remembered Hope, meaning she was very sharp and not easily fooled.

In a way, she was a judge, a harsh one, but not of the troubled often unwed mothers that sat before her as one might think, but rather of the prospective parents.

Not only were these parents expected to adhere to a strict set of rules put forth by her, they also had to raise their new child in the Catholic faith and attend one of its parochial schools. If these erstwhile mothers and fathers passed preliminary inspection but failed to disclose anything on the application and she found out about it, they were unceremoniously thrown out of the office, the dramatic scene resembling God casting Satan from heaven as depicted in Milton's *Paradise Lost.*

If couples could pass Sister Apollonia's rigorous inspection, most likely they would make excellent parents, and all of Boston knew it.

"No, Sister, I didn't have another child," Hope said as she spied the all-important file cabinet in the corner. "It's my son, Tommy, he is a wonderful boy."

"Well, Miss Davis, I am sure that is true, but I thought you were aware that we have a hard and fast rule that we only take children up to three years of age. If my math is correct, Tommy is well past that age, am I right? Also, you realize the application fee is non-refundable, did I not make this clear to you?"

The application fee was indeed non-refundable, and steep, making the agency a moneymaker for the Sisters of Jesus the Merciful order, which they used for other charitable projects around the world.

"Yes, Sister, I know the rule but..."

Before Hope could say another word there was a scream in the hallway and a crash of something hitting the tile floor.

"My baby!!! Where is my baby?!! I changed my mind!! What have you done with my baby?!!!"

A startled Sister Apollonia excused herself to attend to the commotion, as a cacophony of crying babies added to the drama. The *Clack, Clack, Clack* of Sister Apollonia's shoes against the highly polished hallway floors proclaimed a force to be reckoned with was on the way to bring order to the chaos.

Left alone, Hope worked quickly, opening the top drawer of the well-worn, ominous looking metal file cabinet. For all the money the order spent on renovations, they didn't spend a dime on office furniture, preferring to accumulate an eclectic mix of cast offs donated by other Boston business concerns.

She scribbled down the names, addresses and employment information of the names of four couples towards the front of the file, knowing they had been on the waiting list the longest and probably were the most anxious, not knowing if or when the agency would soon contact them for a final interview. The word around town told a cautionary tale of a number of couples being found out for past indiscretions and being rejected as potential parents at the eleventh hour, so until final papers were signed there were a lot of sleepless nights.

Efficiently completing her task, Hope was putting the file back in its original order when she heard the telltale *Clack, Clack, Clack* of the precipitous approach of the judge, jury and executioner returning to her office. Hope lost her composure, dropping the files and scattering their contents. The *Clack, Clack, Clack* was getting progressively louder, sounding like a ticking time bomb about to go off, making Hope feel like her actions could be responsible for taking down the building and everyone in it. What was she thinking, that this stupid plan would work in the first place?

Hope put the files back as best she could, knowing some couples may have been moved up the list and others down, like the fates had reshuffled the deck, matching different babies with new parents. Feeling another panic attack about to hit her, she returned to her chair just as Sister Apollonia's looming presence filled the room.

"I am so sorry, Miss Davis. Unfortunately, some women have second thoughts, but believe me, all our babies are placed in excellent homes. You look distressed, can I get you some water?"

"Thank you, no, Sister. Where is that person? I don't hear her anymore," asked Hope, fully aware of the hysterical woman's identity, just not her whereabouts.

"Don't worry, some of the sisters escorted her outside and were going for a walk on the Common to settle her down. Again, Miss Davis, maybe you should try another adoption agency. You and your son do not meet our criteria. I'm sorry."

Hope mercifully left the agency and took a detour through Boston Common hoping to catch sight of a disturbed woman being consoled by a couple of nuns, but saw nothing of the sort. Within twenty minutes Hope reached her sister's house, dismissed the babysitter and waited, which to her seemed an eternity. Tommy woke from his nap and came into the parlor.

"Mommy, what's for supper tonight? I'm hungry."

Hope looked at her son with mixed emotions, again not sure if her plan to give him up was the right thing to do. She realized those feelings were nothing new, nearly every parent has second thoughts the rest of their life no matter what the circumstance.

"Boiled pot roast, with potatoes and carrots, your favorite," Hope answered, feeling somewhat guilty, another emotion parents can't seem to shake.

She heard the door open. Ellen was finally home.

"Can you go upstairs and play so I can talk with your Aunt Ellen?" Tommy just nodded leaving the two sisters to talk, which to him, they never seemed to get tired of doing.

"So, how did you do?" Ellen asked brightly, flushed with excitement for her part in the caper.

"I got four names, what took so long? I thought you might have been found out."

"No, everything went according to plan. The two nuns that escorted me out, Sister Ann and Sister Marie were so nice I treated them to ice cream at Bailey's. Then we went to Filene's to see this year's new shoes."

Hope just glared at her sister, obviously taking this whole plan as some kind of adventure, not seeing how upset she was.

"You went shoe shopping with nuns while I'm having a heart attack? Who knew they even liked shoes."

"They're still women, aren't they? They told me something interesting about Sister Apollonia. She is a great violinist, professional quality, apparently. Whenever there is a stormy night and the children are afraid, she plays classical music and it quiets them right down and they go to sleep. She also claims that kind of music helps their brains develop. Crazy, right?"

"Ellen, let's get back to the plan, okay? These people on the list all are going to have final interviews so we have to move fast."

"You're right, let's check them out. I'll put on a pot of coffee."

For the next two hours the sisters parsed the names that Hope had written down, making a list with positives on one side and negatives on the other. The entire exercise of being able to pick out a new potential father for Tommy was unusual for Hope, to say the least, given the fact that both her children's biological fathers arrived at that esteemed position strictly by accident and weren't even aware they had children with her.

Now, here she was, picking a new father for her son from a piece of paper.

The sisters eventually eliminated the first and second families on the list, reasoning their final interview could happen before Hope reached out to them and Sister Apollonia might catch on to their scheme. It was close between the third and fourth couples, but the sisters used some unique reasoning in picking the fourth family.

The third couple was "Ames" and the fourth, "Doyle." They both agreed to go with "Doyle", using logic that would not even be considered in Boston a few years ago: "The Irish are coming on strong, they are going to own this town soon, the old Yankees had their day but are on the way out. Let's go with an Irish family." And to a lesser degree, "This Dennis Doyle is a prosecutor, which sounds like a good steady job and not very dangerous. Tommy is going to need a job someday and businesses come and go but there will always be bad people in the world."

It was settled. A decision that might change the potential futures of hundreds, maybe even thousands, of people that could be born into this world in the future was decided by two sisters over a pot of coffee.

Chapter Four

Dennis Doyle

"Next case, The State of Massachusetts vs. David Van Trap. The Honorable Judge Gerard O'Neill presiding. All rise," the bailiff of Suffolk County District Court announced, filling the vaulted space of the courthouse with his authoritative baritone.

Judge O'Neill, and the prosecutor in this case, Dennis Doyle, were long-time friends that first met when attending parochial school together back in the day. They were well aware they had each gotten a golden ticket into their profession based on their country of origin, something that never would have happened a few years ago in Boston, and they were not about to squander their big break.

Although they may have gotten a good start based on their nationality, their profiles had risen steadily in the legal community based solely on their diligent work, and people outside of the courthouse began to take notice. Importantly for men in their position, both had an innate sense to read which direction the political winds were blowing, and the weather vane in Boston was turning from Republican red to Democratic blue, and most fortunately for them, Emerald green.

Their futures were bright and they knew it.

"Mr. Van Trap, is it? Do you go by more than one name?" Judge O'Neill asked, peering over his reading glasses.

"Not currently," Van Trap mumbled.

"Not currently, what?"

"Not currently... your Honor," Van Trap responded icily, swallowing hard.

God, I hate the Irish. 'A potato-eating' prosecutor and judge on my case? This town is going to hell, he mumbled to himself.

"What say you, Mr. Doyle?"

"Well, Mr. Van Trap has been charged with breaking and entering and in possession of a Class D substance, heroin. This is his eighth offense, your Honor. I recommend the State sentence Mr. Van Trap to nine months in the Charles Street jail."

"Nine months!! That's not right! I'm getting railroaded here," Van

Trap spewed.

"I apologize for my client's outburst, your Honor," stated his court appointed attorney. "The sentence does seem a bit harsh."

"Can you explain to the court your reasoning, Mr. Doyle?" asked Judge O'Neill, already well aware of the answer to his own question.

"Well, your honor, Mr. Van Trap unfortunately is a victim of drug abuse which fuels his life of crime and will go on indefinitely unless this cycle is broken. There is a chaplain at the Charles Street Jail that has a voluntary program for inmates based on self-esteem, proper nutrition and exercise and I have seen remarkable results from those that took advantage of it. It's more a rehabilitative than punitive model. If Mr. Van Trap takes advantage of the opportunity afforded him and takes part in the program, I would be willing to offer him probation in six months."

"You make a compelling argument, Mr. Doyle, I see the merit of your logic. I hereby sentence David Van Trap to a sentence of nine months in the Charles Street Jail pending a review by Mr. Doyle and myself for a possible reduced sentence of six months. Next case," as the gavel sharply reverberated through the courtroom signaling end of all discussion.

David Van Trap stood before O'Neill and Doyle for a moment and said no words, but his venomous stare said volumes. He was then unceremoniously escorted out of the courtroom by the bailiff, the revolving door of the courtroom immune to all manner of human drama, already turning its attention to the next case.

The following Saturday O'Neill and Doyle attended to other pressing matters of the world, trying to beat each other's brains out playing their weekly match at Wollaston Golf Club in Quincy.

Dennis was longer off the tee, but Gerry had a better short game and both men took delight in pointing out the weak parts of each other's game. They usually played as a foursome, but when it was just the two of them, the swearing was only tempered by the quality and vehemence of the insults. A stranger or acquaintance would never be allowed to utter anything close to what they said to each other during one of their matches. It was not meant to be taken personally, just their way of decompressing from their high pressure jobs where even the hint of an improper word could have dire consequences.

Sometimes it is a way to express frustration with the game itself, one of the most difficult sports to master, if that is even possible. It is not uncommon to have days when golf completely humiliates a person yet, when it is finally over, they can't wait to set up their next tee time.

In fact, the more you seem to care about golf, the crueler it seems to treat you. Golf is like that girl you have a crush on but who could care less about you, only calling when she is looking for a favor. You get to stay home Saturday night watching golf's yappy dog while golf's out with someone else giving them a hole-in-one.

Dennis and Gerry insulted each other in such a manner that it sounded like they hated each other to anyone that overheard them, but in reality, the opposite was true.

"I'm not giving you that putt, you can kiss my white Irish ass.""Who do you think you are now that you live on Com Ave, you lace curtain Irish bastard.""Don't even think of asking for a preferred lie, you shanty Irish prick."And, "Make sure you put down the right score, you stupid two-boater," were just a few of the more memorable ones.

After the round, which consisted of four hours of rudely offending each other, only stopping temporarily when one of them attempted a shot, they headed back to the clubhouse for lunch.

The waitress brought over a couple of Vienna beers, a local brew that could be considered mediocre at best, but enjoyed the distinct advantage of being the only brand on tap at the club. They both agreed it tasted much better when the company was called Houghton's, but at least it was cold.

"What looks good today on the menu, Mr. Doyle? Or should I say, Assistant District Attorney Doyle."

"What did you just say?"

"I heard your name bandied about at city hall, Dennis. They will be contacting you this week. Congratulations! Not only is the State happy with our work, the political boys also have their eyes on us for running for office in the future if we're interested in going that route, too," O'Neill pronounced proudly, hoisting his beer.

"Thanks, Gerry. This is great timing, with Maura and me trying to adopt a baby and all. Here's to us!"

The two close friends had come a long way and had every reason to feel the world was their oyster, because it was. They both took a hearty pull of beer from their mugs before lifting them in the air, signaling the waitress for another round.

"What looks good today, Gerry? I see they have 'scrod' on the menu. What is 'scrod' anyway?"

"It's like what the English did to us Irish: they screwed us every chance they got. When we got to Boston their buddies the Brahmins tried to keep it up and wouldn't be happy until we were beyond screwed, they wanted us totally 'scrod'."

"Good one, Gerry, but not anymore. Not anymore!"

What had started out a great round at Wollaston was followed by an even better lunch. As the beer began to kick in, Gerry became a touch philosophical, asking,

"Why do you think we keep busting our asses to do such a good job when the fix is in. We're Irish, right? We can just coast along and go with the flow now that we own the ballot box."

"That's an easy one, Gerry, it has to do with the nuns. It's good old fashioned Catholic guilt."

"You're right, the theme for the next round. To Guilt!" The strange salutation shouted out caused a few heads to turn.

As close friends as they were, Dennis purposely didn't fill Gerry in on the visit later that afternoon at his home with two sisters that somehow knew he and Maura were looking to adopt. Dennis smelled a rat, probably from witnessing human nature at its worst day in and day out, figuring the mysterious sisters were trying to offer up a child for adoption just to put money in their pockets. He normally would never agree to such a meeting in the first place but his wife insisted, and she was in no mood these days to be second-guessed in this matter.

He had a great marriage but, like all marriages, it had its challenges. His wife Maura had tried everything available from the best doctors in Boston in an effort to get pregnant, but she, like her twin sister Colleen, could not. Both sisters had been diagnosed with something called congenital endometriosis making them virtually sterile, and this weighed heavily in both households. Both sisters wanted children badly.

Dennis and Maura decided last year their best option was to adopt and had applied some time ago to the Mary Magdalen Adoption Agency after saving up for the large application fee. It seemed like their fate had been in the nun's hands forever, and each week that went by and the lack of news seemed to make them more and more testy with each other.

Then, to further complicate matters in the Doyle household, the strange call came from the two sisters that prompted today's meeting.

When the doorbell sounded and Dennis opened the door he was in for his first surprise of the afternoon. The woman that introduced herself as 'Hope Davis' was not some furtive looking grifter as he had pictured in his mind, but absolutely stunning and dressed in the latest fashion. He noticed she had pulled up in a sharp-looking automobile as well.

She and the Doyle's made their introductions in the parlor, exchanged a few pleasantries and Hope launched into her story. Dennis had witnessed some of the finest lawyers in Boston presenting their cases, but they had nothing on Hope. For the next twenty minutes she was candid, concise, compelling, and most importantly of all, believable. He realized he had come to this meeting with a closed mind, but she was able to persuade him her intentions were legitimate, especially since she had paid the adoption agency two application fees and was looking for no compensation from the Doyle's, just a good home for her son.

Dennis glanced at his wife out of the corner of his eye and knew how she was leaning based on her body language. He took the bold step of breaking the spell by asking, "When can we meet Tommy?"

"Why, right now. He is in the automobile with my sister Ellen. Let me get them both so you can meet them."

Dennis and Maura weren't sure what to expect by this point, but when they first saw Tommy in his sailor suit and he politely shook their hand saying "Hello, sir," and, "Hello ma'am" while looking them straight in the eye, Maura was done. Ellen took Tommy into the kitchen so Hope could talk further with the Doyle's.

Dennis switched to his professional intonation like he was addressing a courtroom, "Well, Miss Davis, this certainly has been a very enlightening afternoon. I think my wife and I have a lot to discuss..."

"What's to discuss, I've already made up my mind," snapped Maura. "We just need to work out a few details."

"But, I..." Dennis started, but was faced down by not one, but two extremely motivated females, quickly realizing he was no match for them. Knowing he was way out of his league, he made an intelligent decision considering the circumstances by drawing on all his years of schooling and experience as an esteemed officer of the court. He shut up.

Maura obtained Hope's contact information and everyone said their polite goodbyes. When their guests departed, Maura announced curtly, "I'm putting on a pot of coffee," followed by the words every man loves to hear, "We need to talk."

For the next three hours they looked at the situation presented them from every angle they could possibly think of and both came to the same conclusion: after scheduling negotiated four "trial sleep overs" to make sure everyone got along, adoption papers, which Dennis could easily arrange, would be signed.

Unless something unforeseen happened, Tommy Davis would soon become Tommy Doyle.

Chapter Five

Heat Wave

"Mommy, I'm hot. I can't sleep," Tommy Doyle whispered, waking his mother by tugging on her nightgown sleeve around 10 p.m. on July 4, 1911. The Northeast was in the grip of what would be an epic eleven-day heatwave, Boston hitting a record 104 degrees today, but that is not why this date would be forever etched in Maura Doyle's memory. It was the first time her adopted son called her "Mommy".

"Let's go to the kitchen and get some water," she answered quietly. "Daddy's still asleep." In the kitchen, she broke the news to Tommy.

"Your father and I were going to keep this a surprise, but guess where we are going tomorrow?"

Tommy had already been through major changes in his life in his short time on this earth, but because he felt so at ease living in the Doyle household, any new situation he was presented with was now met with simple childhood curiosity, not fear that was an unfortunate product of insecurity. "Where, Mommy?"

"Cape Cod. Your father found a place for us to stay on Lake Wequaquet called Camp Opechee near Craigville Beach. Aren't we the lucky ones?"

"What's a 'Cape Cod'?" Tommy asked, never hearing that term before, not even attempting 'Wequaquet' or 'Opechee'.

"Oh, it's beautiful there. There are beaches, like the one at the lake where we are staying and the ocean, which are the best places to cool off on a hot summer day. And fish, and clams and crabs that just can't wait to bite the toes of a little boy like you!" as she grabbed Tommy's toes, setting off a laughing jag between the two of them, waking up Dennis.

"What's all the ruckus in here," he said in a booming voice as he entered the kitchen, the air stuffy and still but its occupants lively.

"Oh, nothing," answered Maura innocently, "Unless you're looking for a late night snack of toe sandwiches!" which started the two of them giggling again.

He took it all in, that sound of laughter in a household that had deteriorated into a series of tense silences before Tommy came on the scene. In all the years he had known Maura, he never remembered her more content and still couldn't believe how well this adoption had worked out, for everyone.

"Come to think of it, I'm pretty hungry, I could go for a stinky toe sandwich myself!" Dennis bellowed, getting in on the joke, grabbing his son and lifting him over his head. The three of them laughed a bit more before settling down, changing focus to enthusiastically discuss their trip to the Cape. By 11:00, when the yawns signaled the end to this impromptu family meeting, they headed back to their beds, looking forward to dreaming of their upcoming family vacation.

∞

David Van Trap's introduction to the Charles Street Jail was being tossed into a six by eight concrete box, the administration's crude version of a rehab facility, for a week to allow his body to detoxify from his addiction to heroin and the other mind-numbing opiates he had used frequently.

It is one of life's ironies, the pain from one body part that people tried to avoid by taking opioids in the first place, paled in comparison to the excruciating pain their entire body had to endure when coming off drugs, and Van Trap had been an addict for years.

After seven days of sweating, retching and writhing pain, the first three days feeling like he was going to die and the last four wishing he had, his liver somehow managed to clear his body of drugs, and for the first time in years.

With his mind finally lucid, Van Trap spent most of his waking hours not thinking of how he might turn his once promising life around, but conspiring how to be released early from this hellhole.

Of all the places to endure a heatwave in Boston, the Charles Street Jail had to be among the worst. Conditions in the tightly crammed house of incarceration deteriorated quickly as the summer heat and humidity began to take its toll. Packed in like cattle headed to the slaughterhouse under normal circumstances, the historic heatwave Boston was experiencing made life in this dilapidated lockup nearly unbearable for the inmates and not a whole lot better for the guards.

"Shut the hell up! Stop your bellyaching or I'll give you something to really bitch about," hissed David Van Trap at his moaning cellmate, making sure he was out of earshot of the guards in the stifling pressure cooker that was the Charles Street jail.

No doubt it may be hotter in hell than it was in this jail, but it probably smelled better.

Bodily function odors clung to the oppressively humid air, stirring up already violent convicts and adding to the tension, making the confines feel more like a cage full of agitated animals than a house of correction for human beings.

Van Trap continued to scheme, figuring a way to use the current disgusting conditions in this nauseating place to work in his favor, and came up with a plan. As most of the other inmates were acting out and random acts of violence were a daily occurrence, he would be the model prisoner, like he was fully rehabilitated.

Van Trap would be noticed by not being noticed.

Maybe those stupid Irishmen will think they fixed me and let me out early, he chuckled to himself.

∞

Less than a mile away another person was dealing with the heatwave inside a Boston building, this one far different than the one David Van Trap found himself in. Hope Davis spent another day in The Boston Public Library, an architectural gem whose spacious design gave it an uplifting, liberating feel. Several well-placed fans kept the air moving, although Hope was so engrossed in her studies she never noticed the heat, anyway.

"Miss Davis, I'm sorry. The library is about to close."

Hope looked up from her Latin book, her head spinning from absorbing declensions and new vocabulary words. It had only been ten days since she had met with the person in charge of the Latin School for Girls and she already felt overwhelmed by her assignment.

∞

Hope had contacted Penelope Hinckley, the headmistress, and

asked her to lunch, giving the administrator a short version of her life story. Hope then asked if there were any program she could take that would result in granting her a high school diploma so that possibly she could be accepted to a college someday.

Mrs. Hinckley patiently listened to Hope, still a young woman but well past high school age, and her immediate thought was,

Her request is just a crazy pipe dream. She is wasting my time.

"I'm sorry Miss Davis, but I am a very busy woman and I have worked very hard to give my school recognition and credibility. If I..." stopping in mid-sentence, frozen by that look. Hope had that expression on her face that Penelope had seen and experienced herself many times, of people having their mind made up about you no matter what you said or knowing all the facts.

Penelope reminded herself that if Robert Tarpey of the Boston Latin School had shut her off that day when she approached him years ago she wouldn't be headmistress today.

Just as a person's life can drastically change in a heartbeat from an accident or health crisis, so it can by the simple act of someone giving them a chance. Penelope's family knew all about lucky chances.

"On second thought, I have an idea. Before I invest a great deal of time honoring your request, I have to be convinced you are a real student. I am going to give you a Latin test in one month's time to see if indeed you have academic aptitude. Your score will determine your fate."

Hope sat silent for a moment before asking,

"Latin? Like the language?"

"Exactly. The Boston Public Library has some very good books on the subject. I know, I donated them."

∞

A preoccupied Hope exited the library walking out into bustling Copley Square and was immediately hit with a wave of hot, stale air resembling more of what was expelled from a blast furnace than the usual sea breeze that normally tempered the Boston summers. Willis Carrier's invention of modern air conditioning would not revolutionize American households until the 1930's, until then, people had to suffer through oppressive heat and humidity as best they could.

Her mind continued to drift, recalling the article in *The Boston Globe* telling of over three thousand people sleeping on Boston Common in a desperate attempt to get some relief, of horses dying, and sections of pavement becoming pools of molten tar. A number of people that slept on rooftops had fallen to their deaths in the middle of the night, adding to the somber death toll.

It warned that children and the elderly were particularly vulnerable to the heat, and she wondered how Tommy was faring.

Chapter Six

It's All Good

"Mommy, Daddy, watch me! Watch me," squealed Tommy Doyle as he jumped into the pristine waters of Lake Wequaquet, probably for the hundredth time, his parents wondering if he ever got tired. Every day he continued to come out of his shell, revealing an inquisitive, outgoing little boy that treated life like one big adventure.

While the heatwave simmered the residents in Boston, the Doyle's enjoyed the climate on the Cape, nearly always a good ten degrees cooler than Boston in the summer. The only simmering the Doyle's experienced involved lobsters and clams at a seafood restaurant in Harwich.

Dennis picked this spot after being advised the best way to enjoy lobster was outside at a picnic table as the experience could get messy. He chose a two-and-a-half pounder for himself, the recommended perfect size, and slightly smaller ones for Maura and Tommy, making sure the crustaceans had hard shells. Although more difficult to open, he was assured it would be worth any extra effort as they had better texture and taste than soft shelled lobsters which recently molted.

Dennis got excellent advice. It took nearly an hour of cracking open shells, sometimes even resorting to a hammer, finding the precious meat in unexpected places, making the experience for the Doyle's more than just a meal, but like a delicious treasure hunt.

Once they were comfortable eating their lobsters, Dennis knew he could no longer put off the inevitable: someone had to eat the first steamed clam. Being the father and a former cop, he bravely volunteered.

He asked for help on the proper technique, which consisted of removing "the sock from the foot", dipping the clam in brine to wash off any sand, and then dipping it once more in melted butter before it went "down the hatch." He was more than pleasantly surprised at how good it tasted.

His enthusiastic reports were enough for skeptical Maura and Tommy to try one and they, too, were amazed at something so ugly could taste so good. They finished the bucket with gusto.

Despite wearing bibs, juice from the succulent seafood did manage to squirt all over them, making them see the wisdom of eating outside. When they got back to the hotel they all took a dip in the fresh clean waters of Lake Wequaquet, already figuring when they could return to the restaurant for a repeat performance.

They continued to do their Cape vacation in style, taking advantage of the sandy peninsula's many offerings. Besides spending hours at Lake Wequaquet swimming, fishing and canoeing, they also enjoyed the ocean. Craigville was their home beach but they also made a day of it at Mayflower Beach in the town of Dennis on the bay side, searching for tide pool creatures at its trademark low tide, which seemed to go out as far as the eye could see.

Recently appointed Assistant District Attorney Dennis Doyle called in a few favors and was able to play golf twice at Hyannisport, once at Wianno, and the family even took the ferry to Martha's Vineyard for a day. Everyone was enjoying themselves so much he booked the place for the same time next year.

After a fun-filled two weeks, relaxed and more sunburned than they should be, the Doyle's headed back to a much cooler Boston, thunderstorms finally having broken the back of the deadly heatwave.

∞

"Okay, Van Trap, get your stuff. You've been let out early."

This is exactly what Van Trap wanted to hear, what he had planned for the last two months. He quickly collected his personal belongings without even a goodbye to his cellmate before hearing that long-awaited metallic *Click!* of the guard unlocking his cell.

"We'll see you soon, Van Trap, I don't buy your act for a minute. I've seen them come and go around here and I'm sure about one thing: you'll be back."

"There is one thing I absolutely guarantee. David Van Trap will never see the confines of the Charles Street Jail again. I guarantee it," Van Trap proclaimed as he walked past the guards.

I guarantee it because from now on I'm going back to my old name. David Van Trap is dead as far as you're concerned, you dirty screws! mumbled Duncan Troupe as he strutted with his head held high, into the Boston sunshine.

∞

"Miss Davis, I have to confess, I wasn't entirely convinced you were serious about your studies but these test results prove your ability," Penelope Hinckley beamed, handing Hope a first year mid-term Latin test with a "92" and an outsized "A" encircled at the top of the page. "Congratulations."

"Thank you, Mrs. Hinckley," Hope said, wondering which answers she had gotten wrong.

"Miss Davis, please call me Penelope, can I call you Hope?"

"Yes, thank you... Penelope."

"Hope, how would you like it if I acted as your mentor? I can design a curriculum for you and come up with some sort of exam to prove you are capable of graduating from a Massachusetts high school. What do you think?"

"I have a daughter so I will have to juggle things a bit. Fortunately, we moved in with my sister and she has been very supportive, so yes, I am saying 'yes' to your generous offer."

"If something comes up I understand, but for now I would like to meet with you once a month and I will test you on the previous month's work. Are you up for this challenge?"

"Yes, Penelope, I believe I am."

Truth is, wild horses couldn't stop me now.

Chapter Seven

Reunion

Duncan took a deep breath before walking up the path to the impressive Troupe family home in the elegant town of Brookline, Massachusetts for the bittersweet reunion with his father, Fredrick. The lawn and landscaping were, as always, perfectly manicured and the home meticulously maintained, giving neighbors and passers by the feeling its occupants led a well ordered and harmonious life.

Duncan had let his hair grow back out and shaved his beard to help convince himself David Van Trap was just someone he used to know from his past.

That was all just a phase, a youthful indiscretion.

Duncan stood for a moment staring at the massive front door emblazoned with '**Troupe**' in large brass lettering, wondering if this slab of oak had been more successful over the years keeping prying eyes out or family secrets in.

It stirred up thoughts of his mother, a subject on which his father had forbade discussion since he was a young boy, whose very name risked bouts of Fredrick's rage-filled corporal punishment. Hazy memories of his mother, her extended stays in psychiatric hospitals, prolonged periods of bedrest, doctors convening in hushed tones in their parlor, of her goodbye to him before she ended her agony with a handful of medication, flooded his mind.

Duncan remembered his father telling someone it all started when she gave birth to him, that she was perfectly fine before he came along, wondering if that was why his father…

No, that is all ancient history. All that matters are here and now, expelling such thoughts using his usual coping mantra.

Duncan sighed, rang the bell and was escorted by the maid through the entry hall on the way to a new addition to the already sprawling home, a solarium. As was his habit, he briefly stopped in front of a mirror to adjust his tie, took two steps away and returned to brush his hair, admiring himself for the fine figure he cut.

He recalled the ferocious argument he had with his father his last time here and he wasn't quite sure how his father would receive him this afternoon.

The maid directed him to the sunroom chock full of an eclectic mix of plants, obviously not cultivated for their esthetic appeal, but more for the precious oxygen they created. The solarium overlooked the swimming pool whose sparkling waters looked inviting on this warm October day, but probably hadn't seen use in years.

Again, without the mind-numbing effect of drugs in his system, memories bubbled up into his consciousness. Such as that period beginning when he was ten and lasting several years when a series of heartbreaking drownings of family pets occurred in this very swimming pool. Tragic, truly tragic.

Duncan snapped out his daydream when the private duty nurse pushed the wheel-chair bound Fredrick Troupe into the sun splashed room.

"Father, how wonderful to see you again. I bet you are surprised to see me," Duncan said, employing that confident tone all children of privilege seem to possess, extending his hand. Once a strong, vigorous man, emphysema from years of ignoring his doctor's pleas to quit smoking left Fredrick a frail and much smaller version of his former self, now struggling for each precious breath.

Duncan felt the lack of vigor shaking his father's bony hand, the very one that struck him repeatedly as a child, often disciplining him for things he never fully understood. Sometimes it was an open-handed slap, other times a closed fist hit, always with that damned right hand.

Now I could crush that hand like an egg, old man. It might help us even the score.

In contrast Duncan looked to be on top of his game, not at all what Fredrick was expecting based on the last report from his private investigator, Mike Stusse.

That dick must be losing his touch, Fredrick mused. *He assured me Duncan was strung out on drugs, a lost cause. One thing's for certain, Stusse's not getting another dime of my money.*

"You look to be in outstanding shape, Duncan. I was led to believe otherwise," the deliberate words expressed with great effort.

"I was fortunate to enter an outstanding facility that specializes in restoring people like myself that had slipped. In fact, it is such an impressive program many of my fellow colleagues are still there. Not only am I feeling in the best shape of my life from exercising and eating healthier, I am fully ready to enter the family business."

Ha! I'm so smart. I'm glad I used Van Trap as my name in court. By the time my father puts two and two together it will be too late.

The Troupe men guardedly conversed for the next half hour, like two cagey boxers in a rematch circling the ring, each wanting a piece of the other while keeping their guards up. Fredrick knew a lot more of Duncan's recent history then he let on, but, due to his failing health, uncharacteristically gave his son the benefit of the doubt.

Fredrick took measure of his only son, the same son that had bitterly disappointed him so many times in the past. But somehow the Duncan in front of him looked exactly like every father wanted his son to look, as if he could conquer the world while carrying forward the family name.

If he was in this kind of shape when he was at Harvard, he could have stayed on the football team. The coach would never have let the dean kick out a strong player like Duncan for his 'minor indiscretion'.

Fredrick made a mental note to call his attorney and restore Duncan in his will as the sole heir of his estate, inheriting the business and his vast real estate holdings, which instantly would make Duncan one of Boston's richest men on paper.

The other part of Fredrick's estate plan was back in play as well. One quarter of his cash, a princely sum, was to be utilized in Duncan's behalf in a special capacity he would never find out about.

Seeing Duncan in his current state of health reminded him what those charlatan psychiatric doctors had warned him about when he was young.

What did they say about Duncan again? That he had 'narcissist tendencies', what does that even mean? Split personality? Sociopath? Bat-shit crazy? What the hell do they know? The medical community failed my wife and failed me... they're just a bunch of inept quacks.

Although Fredrick's physicality faded more every day, his mind remained fairly sharp and at this stage of his life he wanted what all rich old men wanted, their family name to be immortalized. Some men put their names on hospital wings or parks, but Fredrick's aspirations were much higher, he wanted the Troupe name in the history books.

He needed to find out if his sole heir had a change of philosophy and decided to test his son.

"Well, Duncan, what do you think of how the Irish are taking over Boston? Something like this could only happen in America, right?"

Duncan got red in the face, pronouncing,

"If I had anything to do about it, any of them here that aren't citizens yet would be rounded up, sent back and no more would be let in. Boston was much better under the Brahmins. I hate all immigrants, but especially the Irish."

Most fathers would cringe if their son spewed out such racist hate speech, but for Fredrick it was exactly what he wanted to hear, it made him feel proud. His son may have been expelled from Harvard but he had learned the lessons his father taught him well.

The next call after his attorney would be to the 'organization' informing them he was sending a fat check with very specific strings attached. It was a call he was looking forward to for years.

Now, if I only had a grandchild…

Chapter Eight

Touching Base

"May I ask who's calling, sir?"

"This is Judge Gerard O'Neill. Do you know when Mr. Doyle will be available?"

"I'm sorry, Your Honor, it's been a while since I heard your voice. Mr. Doyle is on the other line. Is there something I can help you with?"

"No, thank you, it is something of a personal nature. I am in my chambers and will be awaiting his call. Goodbye."

After ten minutes or so, Dennis returned his call.

"Aren't we high and mighty now, Mr. Doyle? It wasn't that long ago that you answered the phone yourself," Gerry not wasting any time tearing in to his best friend. "I was wondering if we could hit the links at Wollaston Saturday. This November weather has been pretty warm, perfect for a golf. Besides, I need someone to pay for my beer."

"Great to hear from you, Gerry. I wish I could say yes but the 'Young Democrats' are having a luncheon Saturday so I have to beg off. You probably would clean my clock anyway because I haven't touched a club in, I don't remember when. The price of success, a high handicap."

Gerry was disappointed but didn't let on.

"I have a whole new string of insults and swears I want to try out on you, Dennis. It's one of the fringe benefits of being in this business, being exposed to different aspects of the English language."

"That I'm sure of. How's the family?"

"Oh, the kids are great, Fiona got that flu going around, she still isn't quite back yet."

"Sorry to hear that. Give her our best."

"I will, how's it going with Tommy?

"Really well, it's like he was part of the family from the very start."

"That reminds me, I've got a contact that can score tickets for you, me and Tommy at that new Fenway Park for opening day next year. It always amazes me how many people happen to get sick or have that aunt that always seems to die in Boston on opening day. Quite a coincidence."

"That sounds great, Gerry. The 1912 club should be really good, maybe they could win it all. No pitcher in the league is better than Smokey Joe Wood, he's the difference, for sure. I tried to see the Sox play for the last time in their old park but couldn't, being so damn busy, thanks to you."

Judge Gerard O'Neill spent his entire day carefully choosing his words lest he offend someone in the slightest or they took what he said out of context. Every word he said had to be perfectly parsed knowing every syllable he uttered was liable to be second-guessed and possibly causing a legal or political outcry. Keeping the importance of his words to his best friend in mind he knew exactly how to respond:

"Asshole!"

"Right back at you, shithead!" as both men broke into hearty laughter.

Judge O'Neil's secretary knocked on his door and popped her head in, drolly announcing,

"The jury is back in the courtroom with their verdict, your Honor," and just as quickly took her leave.

"Dennis, I have to go, the jury is in. I still wish we could play golf before it gets too cool."

"Me, too, Gerry. Don't worry, we are still young and have all the time in the world. Remember what we talked about when we retire? We will be those old farts that play every day so we can get the cost of our memberships down to twenty-five cents a round. They will hate our guts! We have the whole rest of our lives to play."

"Yes, still… talk to you soon, I've got to go."

With that the Judge put on his robe and went back to the business of trying to sort out the mystery of how and why human beings, capable of beautiful art and incredible acts of kindness, could also perpetrate heinous crimes and do such despicable things to one another.

People never ceased to amaze him.

∞

The hall was jam-packed and crackling with energy. A new, young face of The America Only Party was going to address the crowd tonight and everyone was energized.

"I would like to introduce to this extraordinary gathering this evening a special guest, Duncan Troupe. Mr. Troupe, would you kindly say a few words for us."

Duncan made his way to the lectern, looking all the part of a successful politician. Always carefully groomed and well dressed, he spent more hours than usual in front of the mirror this week practicing his speech. Every hair was in place and his clothes were tailored to perfection.

"I would like to say first off, 'Thank you', for such a wonderful turnout tonight." Wild applause from about fifty members of the crowd served to prime the pump and energize the others.

"Thank you, thank you," Duncan said raising his hands to quiet the crowd. He felt all eyes on only him and everyone listening to his every word and he loved it. And the cheers, it was a rush that was nothing quite like this for him, except maybe that first shot of heroin.

"You know, folks," Duncan now feeling it, "It's pretty simple actually. Immigrants are ruining our fair city of Boston, especially those Catholics from that island near England," to wild applause. He spoke in a commanding yet folksy manner the crowd seemed to relate to.

These are my people and it's like I'm touching them with my words.

"I promise you one thing if I am your candidate to represent The America Only Party, I will make Massachusetts great again!" Earsplitting clapping followed by a band playing *The Star Spangled Banner* brought the crowd to a frenzy.

Not everyone in the room was quite so boisterous. Two older gentlemen in the back calmly surveyed the scene and simply took it all in.

∞

Hope figured the mild November afternoon might draw them to Boston Common, and sure enough she spotted them, keeping her distance just enough as not to be noticed. She tried to stay away, but the longest she was able to was two weeks.

Then as if on cue, a young boy picked up a stick and gleefully chased a squirrel up a tree, hitting the trunk as the squirrel chattered his disapproval. She had witnessed this scene many times, noticing he never seemed to tire of it, and neither did she.

Seeing Tommy so happy, I'm positive I did the right thing.

Watching her son play on the Common was as close a connection to him Hope would allow herself, honoring her agreement with the Doyle's to not be part of his life. He was obviously thriving which made her feel happy, but inadequate at the same time, and perhaps even a little guilty. Maybe if she'd just given it more time things would have worked out differently.

No, I'm pretty sure I did the right thing.

There went Tommy again, running at full tilt, did this boy ever get tired? As he circled around a large elm he tripped over a root, scraping his palms as he broke his fall. At first he appeared startled and then started to cry. Maura ran over making sure he was not badly hurt, hugging him as she brushed his hair. Just as quickly he collected himself, shaking off the mishap and was soon off again.

That should have been me consoling him. Did I do the right thing after all?

Chapter Nine

The Kingmakers

"What did you think of Troupe's debut last night?" Herm Pottle asked Phil Lockhart at their usual breakfast spot near the top of Beacon Hill, a pitching wedge away from the Statehouse. They were the two seasoned political operatives standing in the back of the hall that were surprised at the excitement the new candidate under their watch generated.

"Not bad, surprisingly. I expected those guys we hired to clap and cheer but he had the whole room going. And that, 'Make Massachusetts Great Again', was that yours?"

"No, I swear, that was all him, kind 'a catchy, too. I think this boy might be a natural," Herm pronounced. Being a veteran hired gun like Phil, he didn't say things like this lightly. It seems like they had worked for them all, Republicans, Democrats, and what was this one, The America Only Party or some such bullshit? It didn't matter to them as long as the check cleared.

"So, what do we really know about this guy? The more of his dirty laundry we get to see before the press the better."

"I'm with you, that's why I hired Mike Stusse, you remember him. It seems he had done a lot of work for the old man but got himself fired, so I figured if anyone was motivated to find dirt on the Troupes it would be Stusse. I also think we need to keep him on the payroll for the foreseeable future, he knows too much."

"Good thinking. What's the deal?"

"Let's take them one at a time and get our stories straight so we'll be ready when the reporters ambush us. First, the old man put him back in the will so Duncan is now filthy rich and some people will be jealous."

"No, that just means he doesn't need anybody's money, he is above reproach, can't be bought. The only reason he is running is to give back because he loves Massachusetts."

"Not bad. Next, he got kicked out of Harvard but they were able to keep it hush-hush."

"Mr. Troupe decided to leave Harvard feeling it was elitist and run by radical left wing professors that Duncan saw as anti-American."

"Got it. Stusse says after Harvard young Troupe got caught up in drugs. He was *persona non grata* for a while. One good thing, apparently the old man gave Stusse enough cash to be able to get Troupe's court records 'misplaced'."

"We have to keep this one under wraps, but if they find out we will say 'how tragic the drug problem is for America's youth, and that with the help of God you can find your way back. Duncan knows this first hand, it happened to him'. Americans love a good comeback story, especially when God is mentioned."

What the two savvy political operatives didn't know was Duncan Troupe wasn't the only one *persona non grata* at the time when Troupe's college experience came to an end. Mike Stusse, who made most of his money catching skirt chasers in the act, chased and caught the wrong skirt himself and got into some serious hot water. By the time Troupe finished serving his sentence in the Charles Street Jail, Stusse returned to Boston from his extended "vacation" in Center Harbor, New Hampshire, leaving major gaps in each man's resume.

"Stusse dug up school records when Duncan was a child and there was a lot written by counselors worried about his mental health, especially when his mother committed suicide. They strongly recommended needed treatment but the old man always refused," Pottle offered.

"We have to keep this quiet, too. Maybe this has something to do with Fredrick blaming the Irish Catholics for everything that is wrong with the world. That's a hell of a lot easier than looking at himself. The old man is as sick a bastard as the kid."

"I agree, the only difference is the Troupes are loaded, and we both know if you have enough money in the good old U.S. of A. you can get away with just about anything. Duncan is definitely loony, but it's not like he killed anyone or anything."

"What about the ladies? Any woman problems in the past?'

"None that we know about. The only thing that stands out is Duncan will not be seen with a woman unless she is absolutely beautiful. Some women might think he doesn't care what they think as long as they look good, like they were just an object, or something."

"Who cares, they can't even vote, anyway. Besides, you and I both know Americans like a good looking first lady."

"That's about all that Stusse could drag up that might hurt him as a candidate. I had to laugh when he put in his report: Duncan Troupe has 'a tendency to lie and shows no signs of empathy or remorse for people he may have harmed'. Doesn't that sound like he could be talking about any of the other politicians we have worked with?"

"I couldn't agree more. What do you think of this America Only Party? What's their deal?"

"The America Only Party is nothing more than a re-hash of the old Know Nothing Party, you know, anti-immigrant, anti-Catholic and especially anti-Irish. They want to make the Irish scapegoats, like groups have done with the Jews, blaming them for everything that has gone wrong in the world. They're also very anti-Catholic and want to return to 'the good old days', whatever that means. They have their heads up their asses."

"For their platform?"

"Absolutely, but not for the reasons most people might think. Obviously, this party is run by a bunch of would-be Brahmins who see their power slipping away and are jealous of the new political power the Irish have. Take morals out of it, we both know how the system works, that normally money always rules elections, but this town is different now. It's political suicide in Boston to be anti-Irish, they have most of the votes and have learned how to use them, we ought to know, we helped teach them. This is totally an Irish town now."

"Yeah, the Irish were part of other people's history, now they want to make some history of their own here in Boston. Where does that leave us?"

"The old man gave us access to a big pile of dough, a really big pile, to make his son the face of this so-called America Only Party. All we have to do is string him along and take him for as much money as we can before his son gets into an election when people actually vote. Once that happens he'll get crushed and its game over for us, but in the meantime we can set up some high profile appearances for Duncan from time to time just to keep the fires burning. This should work well unless Troupe actually starts to really believe his speeches and gets carried away with himself. We are going to have to pull back the reins on him like one of those jockeys on the take at Suffolk Downs."

"Remember back in the day when we used to work on campaigns and it was all about getting behind the best candidate and working like hell to get him elected? Hugh O'Brien, now there was a guy, first Irish Catholic mayor of Boston. The Brahmins threw everything they had at him but we still were able to organize his fellow Irishmen to get him elected. Remember the 'comb trick'?"

"Do I, that was a beauty, taking out teeth of a comb so when they lined it up on the ballot it showed exactly who to vote for. All Irish candidates including O'Brien, naturally. Even people that didn't know how to read got it right."

"Yeah, and O'Brien fooled all of us by doing such a good job he got elected for a second term, to boot. Even some Brahmins voted for him the second go around."

"Yeah, because he lowered taxes. Those rich Brahmins would even let their only daughter marry an Irish Catholic if he were able to lower their taxes."

Both men laughed at this one, humor always funnier when there was a ring of truth to it.

"It felt good back then, didn't it? Like we were helping to even the score, that the Irish had been shit on for so long they deserved a break and we helped give them one. The pendulum always swings back and another group that can put together a large block of votes will take the reins, but for now the Irish are running this town. Now, here we are getting paid by those wannabe Brahmin assholes that are trying to put the genie back in the bottle. Sometimes I feel like a total sellout."

"Yeah, I hear you. The political game has changed so much now that there is so much damned money in it. Don't get me wrong, it's there for the taking and I'm not above taking my share, but I think once people figure out how big money is really calling the shots in politics they'll wise up and demand a change. But in the meantime..."

"Yeah in the meantime, let's enjoy the ride. It never lasts, but it's always one hell of a ride."

Chapter Ten

Thanksgiving

"Auntie, your turn to find me!" Tommy Doyle urged Colleen Flynn, Maura's twin sister, to participate in another round of his favorite game, hide and seek.

"Okay, but your mother needs my help in the kitchen. Better hide good!"

Tommy scampered up the stairs heading to his top-secret hiding place. The last time she played he completely stumped her with this clever spot before proudly sharing it with her as long as she promised to keep it hush-hush.

Sure enough, Colleen found him where she expected, but only after calling his name for ten minutes, sometimes hearing him giggling behind the wall in his closet.

After the reveal, the two headed back downstairs for the Thanksgiving feast. A quick rendition of grace was followed by the spirited passing of multiple side dishes and, of course, turkey, the main event.

With all the commotion one dish just sat there as if no one was quite sure what to make of it.

"Well, it looks like no one else is willing to try it, what the heck, I'm game. Pass me that cranberry, uh, whatever you call it," Mike Flynn said of this year's new food product, canned cranberry sauce. The Cape Cod Cranberry Company managed to process cranberries into this convenient form, but the final product did look strange, a red blob taking on the shape of the inside of a can sitting on top of a serving plate.

"Hey, not bad! Not bad at all," Mike giving his approval of the exotic side dish to the gathering. He was a Cambridge cop living on the other side of the Charles River with his wife Colleen, an emergency room nurse at Mass General. Maura and Colleen were very close as twins often are but their husbands also got along as well. It probably helped they both had law enforcement backgrounds.

"You know, Dennis, that boy Tommy of yours has some motor on him. I could see us all at a Thanksgiving high school football game someday cheering him on as he outruns everyone in the fourth quarter making the winning touchdown," Mike added.

"I could see that myself, those games are becoming quite a tradition. Can someone pass me the potatoes?"

Tommy sat up a little taller in his seat, proud the men at the table were talking about him. He didn't know what 'football' or 'touchdown' meant but he was excited to ask his father about it later.

It wouldn't be a Doyle/Flynn get together unless the subject of politics were brought up, this time Maura decided to lob the first volley with, "I really like our mayor, John Fitzgerald. He is doing a lot for Boston, especially the port."

Mike took the bait, joining the on-going lively family discourse, responding, "Honey Fitz? Talk about the gift of the gab, that guy could talk a dog off a meat wagon."

Dennis jumped in.

"Mike, you're in Cambridge, your mayor Barry might not be such a sweet talker as our Honey Fitz, but is still big on putting family and friends on the payroll. The last one you had, McNamee, I thought they were going to put up new signs in Cambridge, "If Not Irish, Don't Bother to Apply," getting a laugh from everybody getting the irony.

What a difference a few decades made, this being a great time to be of Irish heritage in Massachusetts. Between all the union and civil service jobs they had first crack at and the political power they were acquiring, the stories the old timers shared of tough times for the Irish were now regarded as no more than ancient history.

Looking at the spread in front of him, Dennis wondered what his grandfather, the starving Doyle that was victim of the Potato Famine, that landed in Boston would think of all this.

Probably, he would say the same thing I am going to, "Hey, how about some turkey on this side of the table before it gets cold, for crying out loud."

As the afternoon progressed, it was apparent to anyone witnessing Thanksgiving in the Doyle household it had a decidedly celebratory feel to it. The room felt warm and inviting, filled with animated conversations and aromas of delicious food that is usually only served on special occasions. Everyone had a great day.

As people got up from the table to clear the dishes, Dennis pulled Mike aside to remind him, "Don't forget to put those papers in a safe place," referring to the packet of legal documents concerning Tommy he had given Mike earlier. Mike gave Dennis a slight nod, which was enough to satisfy the Assistant District Attorney of Suffolk County.

As the busy day came to a close, plans for the next holiday, Christmas, were discussed.

"There never seems to be enough time between Thanksgiving and Christmas, it goes by so fast, doesn't it? Don't forget, we all meet here Christmas morning to see what Santa brought Tommy. Don't come too late or someone might get antsy," Maura laughed, nodding to her son as she gathered up her guests' coats.

∞

"Mom, can I get you something to drink?" asked Hope Davis, already knowing the answer to her question as well as the drink that would be requested. Ellen and Hope were hosting Thanksgiving for their mother Delores, who they hoped wouldn't get too loaded to ruin the holiday.

"Thank you, dear, that would be wonderful. Bourbon with just a splash of water would fill the bill."

Hope knew bourbon would more than just 'fill the bill' as her mother probably had enough of it in her lifetime to get a good start filling Boston Harbor.

"It's been so long since I've seen my girls," gushed Delores. "I have been so busy. I have a new man in my life named Frank. He was quite well to do until his wife ran out on him and cleaned him out. Sometimes he comes over and after we have a few, we end up having a good cry. He is a swell guy."

They're all swell after a few, right mom? thought Hope as she handed her mother the first tumbler of the day, knowing the sooner the food was served the better as it might help delay the boozy, incoherent version of Delores from entering the scene. Hope watered down her mother's drink with the expectation of a relatively calm holiday for once.

No such luck.

"What's with this drink, you trying to drown me with all this water? Like they say, if you want anything done right, you have to do it yourself. Thanks for nothing," protested Delores as she struggled to her feet, pointing herself in the direction of the bottle.

"Ellen," Hope shouted to her sister in the kitchen, "Let me give you a hand," uneasily leaving her daughter Emily alone with her grandmother.

Better now than when the bourbon really kicks in, Hope thought as she hastily left to help with the food to speed up the process.

As they sat down to their meal, which up until now had been relatively devoid of the usual Davis drama, Ellen announced proudly, "Hope is going to school, Ma. She even took Latin."

"Latin? That's a dead language, isn't it? What are you going to do, talk to ghosts?" Delores chortled.

"What a waste of time! A great looking girl like you could land a rich man in a heartbeat; school is for men or homely girls with glasses. Speaking of glasses, somehow mine appears to be empty, would one of you girls be so kind?"

"Mom, could you slow down a little so we can at least try to have a nice Thanksgiving?" Hope implored quietly.

"What's a matter, now that you know Latin you think you're too good for your mother? I know your story, missy, you're no one to be putting on airs," Delores said, a case of the "slurs" coming on.

This is exactly why Hope hesitated to invite Delores, not for all her insulting, drunken nonsense directed at her, she was used to it, but so Emily wouldn't be exposed to such talk from her grandmother and possibly be influenced by it.

Hope wanted her daughter never to be dependent on a man, liquor, drugs or anything else for that matter. Hope saw education as the key to independence and thus freedom, for both her and Emily.

"Mom, let's change the subject," Hope said, walking on those all too familiar eggshells, trying to keep the peace.

"I see a production called *The Sun Dodgers* is coming to the Majestic around Christmas. Would you like to go, maybe you, me and Ellen?"

"You're just trying to shut me up! I don't appreciate it, not one bit. Get me another one, and make it a good one before I really get upset."

The rest of the meal was held in a tense silence, only broken by the sounds of forks and knives clattering against earthenware plates.

Another fun family get together, Hope thought. *Happy Thanksgiving… again.*

∞

"Good afternoon, Father," Duncan Troupe addressed Fredrick, already perched at the head of the expansive table in the formal dining room. Duncan, all six foot two of him, came to the meal handsomely attired, appearing like someone that spent a lot of time at the tailors keeping up with the latest fashion. Now that he was getting a sizable stipend from his father, he could dress the way he felt he deserved for a man in his position.

It was just the two Troupe men for Thanksgiving dinner in this spacious room that had the feel of a nearly empty baseball stadium playing out the string after another miserable losing season. It's not so much the emptiness as the lack of crowd noise, save for the announcer's voice echoing off empty seats, the vendors' pleas to sell their wares to too few customers, and catcalls from the few disgruntled fans that still bothered to show up. It was far different than that unmistakable audible murmur, like the sound generated from a vigorous beehive, emanating from an excited crowd when the ballpark is packed and the team is on a winning streak.

Duncan took a seat toward the middle of the table, the large room so unnaturally quiet he could hear the *hiss* from his father's oxygen tank. It was too quiet, making him feel uneasy, knowing that was when he could hear *his* voice.

"Duncan," Fredrick gasped, "I heard marvelous things about you and your work with The America Only Party."

"Yes, Father, I must say I was so happy with all the people in Boston when they reached out to me to carry the party's banner. It is quite an honor. What is the main course today, are we going to have turkey?"

"Absolutely not! That's peasant food. We will have a proper meal of prime rib."

The two men sat quietly for a moment, and just as Duncan feared, he heard *The America Only Party is good but what about me?* as if *he* was sitting at the table. Unnerved, Duncan cleared his throat just to break the silence.

"Are you alright, Duncan? I'll ring for some water."

"Thank you, Father, it's just a tickle. What are your impressions of our mayor?"

"Honey Fitz? Just another Irish political hack, him gushing over that stupid baseball team to boot when he has a city to run. And him having all those children, not one of his children or grandchildren are going to amount to anything, take it from me. God, do I hate those Irish," Fredrick becoming animated, causing a slight gurgling sound.

"Well, Father, you will be happy to know once The America Only Party takes this city back they will be back cleaning houses and digging ditches where they belong and a bunch of them will be leaving Boston, altogether."

"I'm proud of you, Son," words every son wishes to hear from his father even though these were based on hate and racist bigotry.

Again, there was a dreaded quiet period before the food was presented and *he* said to Duncan very clearly,

Get revenge or I will let everyone know about me, including your old man! causing Duncan to say out loud without thinking, "Shut up, Van Trap!"

A confused Fredrick asked, "What did you say? Who is Van Trap?"

"Oh, I'm sorry Father, I was thinking of a heckler at our last rally, some Irish union boss," lied Duncan skillfully from years of practice.

"Van Trap doesn't sound very Irish to me," Fredrick said suspiciously.

"I know, again, it proves you just can't trust those people. Ah, I see the food has arrived. It looks delicious," Duncan happy for the diversion.

The Two Troupes ate their meal with just enough background noise to keep *him* quiet. Duncan knew he would need to attend to the Van Trap side of him before he became a public figure when more eyes besides his father's would follow his every move.

Chapter Eleven

The Argument

Oftentimes when couples are in a social situation and one says something that embarrasses the other, they hold it together long enough until they are alone and then all hell breaks loose. When Duncan Troupe returned home from visiting his father at Thanksgiving, a fight of this nature occurred, but anyone outside the window listening would only hear the voice of one person arguing with his alter ego.

Duncan just barely put his keys on the table when *he* started, *"So, are you happy embarrassing me calling me 'an Irish union boss' to your father?* Van Trap said in Duncan's mind, fuming.

"I can't have you speaking up with people around, they're going to think I'm crazy. My father might be getting suspicious."

You're crazy alright, running around with your America Only Party before taking care of me. I have been here long before the likes of them showed up.

"I thought you liked what they stand for, you know, kick out the immigrants, put the Irish in their place and get rid of the Catholic Church."

I do, but that's about the Troupe name. This is about me, Van Trap. I need action, not just a bunch of words that happen at those rallies. I want revenge, evening the score against your enemies, real or imagined, is the most important thing a real man can do. As far as your father goes, he wants you to be famous so badly he won't hear what he doesn't want to hear.

"Are you still upset about prison? I thought we put all that behind us," Duncan said in an effort to broker a peace with himself.

Of course it's about prison! You already forgot you used my name in court and it was me that went to jail, which ended up protecting your ass. That's so like you, it's always about you, you, you.

"I can't have you just pop into my head every two minutes, I have very important work in front of me. What can I do to make you happy and leave me alone?"

Finally, some action instead of just a bunch of spineless words. Okay, I got the address of that arrogant Irish district attorney, Dennis Doyle, and I have been spying on his house on Commonwealth Ave.

"Is that why I have been having some lost time during the day I can't account for?"

Yes, you idiot, what did you think? If you help me with this I promise I will leave you alone, at least for a while.

A confused Duncan tried to process everything before coming to the realization if he didn't do as the Van Trap part of him asked it could jeopardize his role as the next head of The America Only Party.

"Alright, alright, I'll do what you want. What's the plan?"

That's what I want to hear. Well, Mrs. Doyle almost every day takes her kid out to play on the Common in the afternoon around two o'clock and I checked, she leaves the doors unlocked. I want you and me to get into their house when they're out and take the screws out of the latch in the kitchen window so we can open it on Christmas Eve without making any noise. The paint will keep the latch in place, they won't notice the screws missing.

"You really did investigate the property, didn't you? How did you come up with the idea of taking out the screws from the latch?"

Who says you don't learn anything in prison?

"Okay, I follow you so far, but why are we going back to the house later? On Christmas Eve?"

Remember how shitty you felt about yourself when you got kicked out of Harvard and how disappointed your father was in you? Remember that look he gave you?

"Like it was yesterday. I don't know if a person ever forgets 'that look,'" responded Duncan to Van Trap, his assertive doppelganger.

Exactly. We are going to get that same look but this time we are going to reverse the roles. This time it's Doyle's son that is going to give his father 'that look', like daddy wasn't man enough to protect his own home. We are going to break in on Christmas Eve and steal all the kid's presents and maybe a few of theirs if we have room in our sack. We will be like Santa Claus, but in reverse.

"What if we get caught? I don't want to go back to prison."

Back to prison? Hey, me, David Van Trap went to prison, not you, Duncan Troupe. You owe me on this one. We won't get caught; stop being such a baby, the whole thing should take no more than ten minutes. When the papers get a hold of this they will embarrass the hell out of that Irish bastard. And, there's one more thing.

"Something else, isn't this enough?'

Shut up, stop whining. To do this job I'm going to need a little cocaine to, you know, to give me an edge.

"You want me to score some coke? Where am I supposed to get coke? Coke makes me feel like I can have a heart attack at any minute and keeps me up all night. I stopped doing drugs and alcohol..."

That was your idea, not mine. Don't give me this 'holier than thou' bullshit, you know exactly where to get it. And while you're out and about, don't forget to pick up a big sack. And one more thing.

"Another 'one more thing'?

Shut up. After visiting the old man, I need a nightcap. Make it bourbon, a double, neat.

Chapter Twelve

Never Enough Time

"What did you say again?" Colleen Flynn asked the clerk at the ticket office on Lansdowne Street.

"Five tickets, reserved seats, verses Philadelphia Athletics. A dollar apiece, five dollars total."

"We just want to go to a baseball game, not buy a new car for the players. What day of the week is that game again?"

She had been standing in line for over half an hour on this blustery day to buy Red Sox tickets for the Flynn's and Doyle's for Christmas presents, but she had no idea they cost this much.

"It's a Monday, this is only game left where I can find five seats together. Come on lady, make up your mind, there's plenty of takers behind you. The Sox have a good club and tickets are selling fast. If you don't like the price, well, ball players have to eat, too, you know."

"Okay, okay, I'll take them. Eat, yeah right."

Colleen was a little cranky having worked three doubles in a row which, being Christmas time, were available around this time of year. She and Mike, who also picked up extra details, were scrimping and saving money for the application fee for The Mary Magdalen Adoption Agency, and the couple, if they didn't have quite enough, were getting very close. The possibility of an adoption as successful as her sister's would make all the extra stress worth it.

If I can just hold it together through Christmas, I should be alright when I'll have four full days off and can finally take a breath. I can't wait.

∞

If a person's professional competence had a direct correlation to the neatness of their desk, Dennis Doyle would be judged totally inept instead of the brilliant jurist he was. His desk was constantly a mess.

When he first took this job, his secretary tried to keep his desk neat and orderly, but by the end of the day it was strewn with files in a system only he could understand. Tired of constantly badgering her boss, she gave him an ultimatum: his desk could stay in disarray as long as everyone knew it was all due to him and no reflection on her, and inevitably, when gravity took over and the files hit the floor, it was time to clean his desk, no excuses.

Naturally, this week of all weeks: avalanche! Dennis already had been coming to the office early so he could take the three days after Christmas off, and now this. But, a deal is a deal and he would honor the one he made with his secretary.

Boy, am I exhausted. This job is taking me away from my family a lot more than I thought it would. I can't wait for those days off next week, it's been too damn busy.

∞

"Mommy, have I been a good boy?"

"Yes, Tommy, you have been a very good boy."

"That means Santa will leave me presents, right?'

"Yes," Maura suppressing a laugh, "He most certainly will."

"Great! Can you read *The Night Before Christmas* again? Please?"

Maura, who could probably recite it by heart at this point, responded, "Okay, but the babysitter is coming in a few minutes. I have some last minute shopping to do."

She had every present accounted for except for one: a football for Tommy. After looking all over Boston, she had an epiphany. *They play football at Harvard, let me try there.*

Her sister lives in Cambridge and did the legwork, tracking down a trainer who would have one available this afternoon at 2:30. He would wait for Maura outside the new Harvard Square subway station but only for ten minutes. It was Christmastime and he had things to do, too.

All this running around is crazy, but Tommy will love a football. I think Christmas used to be better in the old days when it wasn't so hectic.

∞

Duncan Troupe unobtrusively slipped into the grimy bar hard by the waterfront frequented by David Van Trap to nervously buy cocaine, trying his best to disguise himself, going so far as to wear shabby clothes he found in the back of his closet in an effort to not draw attention. It turns out he didn't need to bother, the regulars never bothered to lift their heads, far more intent on staring at their captor, that all important liquid in their glass, than him.

Duncan knew the routine: sit at the bar in a certain seat, order the drink corresponding to the drug you want, in his case Canadian Club for cocaine, plunk down your money and the drugs showed up in a napkin along with your drink.

While we're here, get some heroin, too.

"Shut up," Duncan muttered.

"Did you say something, bub," asked the bartender menacingly, making a move toward his well-worn Louisville slugger.

"No, my mind's on something else, busy time of the year, you know."

Duncan slipped the napkin in his pocket and got up off the sticky barstool, hastily taking leave of the sketchy watering hole.

Are you crazy? You left a perfectly good tumbler of CC on the bar.

"Keep it down, someone might recognize me."

Alright, let's go back to your place and do a couple lines to see if we got our money's worth.

"I don't think that's a good idea, we have to keep our focus on tomorrow night."

Listen, you better do as I ask or I'll blow your cover. Speaking of blow, I hope you bought enough for two.

When Duncan got back to his place, he double locked the door and unwrapped the cocaine, pouring it out, forming a small pile on his glass coffee table. He sat for a minute, hesitating, like a novice skier at the top of the mountain considering taking his first black diamond trail, anticipating the thrill of an awesome run but knowing there was also a good possibility it could lead to a painful toboggan ride down, courtesy of the ski patrol.

As much as Duncan Troupe was hesitant, David Van Trap was insistent.

Let's do this! I can't wait! Let's go!

Duncan sighed, beginning the ritual by pulling out two items from his wallet. He lined up the cocaine carefully into a series of rows using his America Only Party card and rolled a five-dollar note into a tube,

Benjamin Harrison's picture facing out for good luck.

Duncan took a deep breath, exhaled, and lowered his head almost touching the glass as he placed the rolled up note into his nostril. In a ten second span that can take a lifetime to overcome, he inhaled two lines of the powder in rapid succession, then wiped his index finger on the glass, picking up a little leftover powder and rubbed it on his gums.

Ah! What a rush!

Duncan's nasal passages immediately went numb and he could hear the sound of his suddenly rapid and erratic heartbeat in his ears. As the nucleus accumbens of the pleasure center in his brain began to light up like the Christmas tree in the rotunda of the State House and override all the other circuits in his brain, his last coherent thought was: *This was a big mistake.*

David Van Trap didn't feel the same sentiment as his personality became more dominant and Duncan Troupe's faded to the background.

I'm the captain of this ship now, it's about time, Van Trap expressed assertively. *We're going to have some fun tonight for a change. It's a good thing your daddy give you a big allowance, Duncan boy, we're making another trip back to the bar tonight and we won't be ordering just one Canadian Club, if you get my drift. Okay, let's go, I'm ready for another hit.*

Chapter Thirteen

Tuck-a-way

"That should do it, I think we didn't miss anything," whispered Maura Doyle, totally exhausted. Like many young parents on Christmas Eve, children added another layer of obligations at an already extremely busy time of the year, and this was their first Christmas with their son.

It will all be worth it to see Tommy's eyes when he sees his presents in the morning.

"What time are Colleen and Mike coming over? Remember my original idea that we could all make Midnight Mass? Who knew we were going to be this tired. Hopefully we can make the 10:30 Mass tomorrow, but it will be packed. I know it's only 8:30 but we should go to bed," Mike yawned.

"Sounds good," Maura sighed. "Nine o'clock I think I told them, I forget." She felt totally spent but contented.

Who knew I could ever be this happy.

∞

A well-dressed man walked by the Doyle residence again around 9:30 p.m., making a loop on Commonwealth Avenue for the fourth time. His finely appointed attire drew very little suspicion if any passerby happened to see him, looking like a wealthy gentleman that may be returning home to his family after a neighborhood Christmas Eve get together. They would be wrong.

That "gentleman", David Van Trap, had stashed a large cloth sack in the alley next to the home he had targeted for months, after parking his automobile on nearby Essex Street. He may have appeared composed, but in reality there was part of him that was jumping out of his skin.

Troupe and his alter ego Van Trap had been up all night doing cocaine as well as some heroin "to even things out." Van Trap loved the high from cocaine but Troupe became increasingly paranoid as the night wore on, constantly looking out the window for people that

72

weren't there, knowing everything about him and what he was about to do.

It didn't matter, Van Trap was in total control now.

Alright, I can't wait anymore, a squirrelly, strung-out Van Trap thought, looking at his watch again, time reading 10:10 p.m. *Time to teach the Irish a lesson.*

He retrieved the sack and stood outside the kitchen window listening for any activity in the Doyle home. Quiet. Dead quiet.

One more hit for luck, as he poured a little coke on the back of his wrist, inhaling it quickly before dropping the vial.

Shit! There still might be a little in there. Forget it, there's plenty more where that came from. He tested the kitchen window and the home's occupants' fate changed for eternity when it popped open with very little resistance.

He tossed in the sack and climbed in, still very fit from his time in prison. Once he let his eyes become accustomed to the ambient light he crept into the living room.

David Troupe had no say in the burglary of course, but he was as scared as he had ever been in his life. Even though he was in good physical shape, the drugs altered his heartbeat to the point he thought he was about to have a stroke.

Van Trap calmly walked over to the Christmas tree, which had a generous number of presents spread under it.

Someone's not going to have the Christmas they thought, he chuckled. *This shouldn't take very long.*

He went to work, taking the 11" Stiletto switchblade knife, a beauty he bought last night at the bar, from his pocket. He loved the metallic "click" sound it made when the blade sprang open, the sound of power, dominance.

He began to methodically slice the wrapping paper open, discovering a child's toy and automatically placed it in the bag. He continued his revenge by taking a few adult presents that struck his fancy while cutting up any clothes he came across, ruining them.

He picked up an oddly shaped object and slashed open its colorful wrapping revealing a football.

I hate football! Who wants this piece of crap, not us, he sardonically thought as he cast it aside, still bitter about his football experiences at Harvard. The ball skidded across the floor and crashed into the wrought iron fireplace utensils, sending the set crashing to the hardwood floor with an audible, *Clang!*

David Van Trap immediately blamed his other self, Duncan Troupe.

Troupe, you idiot! I told you to just stay out of the way.

Duncan, completely submissive up until now, spoke up to his domineering other half protesting in full voice,

"I told you not to do so much coke! That stuff drives me crazy!"

∞

"Dennis, wake up. I heard a voice in the living room," Maura shaking her husband awake, taking a minute to get his bearings.

"Wha… I didn't hear any…" as the unmistakable voice of a stranger in the house was heard again coming from the living room. "You're right. By the sounds of it there are at least two of them and they're arguing about something. I'm going to check it out."

"Dennis, please be careful."

"Don't worry, I'm sure whoever they are don't have a weapon. All burglars learn at an early age armed robbery has a much longer prison term than simple breaking and entering. Once I turn the light on they'll scatter like cockroaches," he whispered, his last words to his wife before exiting their bedroom.

He reached the living room and hit the switch, getting an excellent view of what appeared to be only one intruder, which was his first surprise. The second was it was someone he recognized.

"You!"

∞

Van Trap was startled by the light suddenly flooding the room, temporarily affecting his eyesight, his pupils still dilated from the cocaine.

He was on his knees with only two presents left to open, when the combination of coke, adrenaline, testosterone, jealousy and visceral hate sent him into a blind rage at the sight of the Irish Catholic man that helped send him to prison.

Van Trap sprang to his feat like a cornered animal, rushing Dennis who barely had enough time to assume a defensive position, to no avail.

In a split second, Van Trap forcibly plunged the Stiletto knife just below the solar plexus of Dennis Doyle, assistant District Attorney of Suffolk County, Commonwealth of Massachusetts, husband of Maura and father of Thomas.

In that split second, his life, and others', were changed forever. Dennis began losing consciousness and succumbing to his injury in a matter of minutes.

Like an outer body experience, Dennis could see what was happening around him, but cruelly, was powerless to move or even talk. He could just watch as Maura ran into the room wielding a pair of scissors, creating a sizable defensive wound on the raised forearm of the startled Van Trap.

No, no, no. Why? Dennis thought, powerless to protect his family. He was lying on his side, eviscerated both physically and psychologically.

Mercifully, he slipped into that state between life and death when memories began to flood his mind like he was watching a movie.

Seeing Maura for the first time… the family vacation on the Cape… golf with Gerry… "Stinky toe san"… before fading to black.

The medical examiner would later document a singular knife wound punctured Doyle's descending aorta, one of the body's largest and most vital blood vessels, causing massive internal bleeding. It was determined to be the only injury inflicted.

Van Trap, already agitated, became infuriated with the addition of pain from his forearm wound and the sight of his own blood. In one move, he grabbed Maura by the hair and sliced her throat, severing the carotid artery, causing blood to spurt all over his exquisite camel hair overcoat, the wrapping paper, and the floor.

Maura Doyle's last thought was wondering if her son was safe, then she felt cold, so cold…

All this mayhem created a great deal of noise, enough to awaken anyone else that happened to be in the house. Even someone sleeping soundly upstairs.

∞

Tommy Doyle's dreams of Santa and playing with new toys were interrupted with unexpected thumps and voices coming from the living room.

It must be Santa! Just like 'The Night Before Christmas' that Mommy read to me. I want to look and see him.

Tommy was wide-awake now, hearing some more strange noises.

That must be his reindeer.

He soundlessly crossed his bedroom floor, thought for a minute, before going ahead with his investigation. He figured it would be something fun to tell his parents and aunt and uncle about in the morning.

I can't wait to see Santa!

He padded down the stairs to the landing where the big mirror was before peeking between the banister on the lower staircase, his heart pounding. As he walked down a couple more steps, Tommy saw him and froze in his tracts.

He saw a man and it wasn't Santa and it wasn't his father. This man had a wild-eyed look on his face and was covered in blood. Christmas paper was strewn about the floor and both his parents were lying on the floor in front of the Christmas tree. They were totally still.

Tommy looked directly into the eyes of the intruder, a murderer that had changed his life forever.

Van Trap stared back, the incredible energy of the contrast between life and death, good and evil nearly created a crack of static energy between them that could light up the city.

This intense confrontation caused David Van Trap to snap. Like Satan being cast out in an exorcism, he retreated to the far reaches of a twisted mind. Duncan Troupe became the dominant personality once again.

"Kid, wait. I know this looks bad but it wasn't me, someone else did this. It was an accident," Troupe said in his best soothing and conciliatory tone.

"Let's talk about this," said the new face of The America Only Party, covered in blood while beginning to feel the throb of pain from his own injury.

Tommy hesitated for a split second before his 'fight or flight response' kicked in and he scampered back up the stairs, heading for his favorite hiding place.

Troupe gathered his faculties. The drugs had fully worn off by now, and he knew there was a good possibility he could still get away with this, just as he always was able to get away with everything his whole life. As long as there were no witnesses, that is.

He made a quick move to chase down the young boy on the staircase but slipped on Maura's blood pooled on the floor, knocking the tree over and slowing him down.

Troupe scrambled to his feet and might have possibly caught up to the young boy but hesitated half way up the stairs, his compulsive narcissistic nature once again overpowering him. He stopped to admire himself in the mirror on the landing, shocked to see the condition of his favorite Cashmere coat. As was his habit, he took two steps away from the mirror before returning, always, to fix his hair.

The delay was enough for Tommy to reach his special hide and seek spot, sliding open the panel at the back of his closet that led to the tuck-a-way, the wedge shaped area in the eaves meant for storage. He slid the door closed, curled into a fetal position with his heart pounding, just before Troupe entered his room.

"Kid," Troupe called out sweetly. "I think Santa left a football with your name on it. Come on out and I'll show you."

Troupe's calm demeanor didn't last long. As Duncan became increasingly frustrated, his behavior changed as Van Trap took over again and gained his former fury. He began a new rampage, tossing furniture, throwing toys and clothing in the air before entering Tommy's closet, now like a wild animal.

Tommy made himself feel smaller and smaller in the cold, dark tuck-a-way, hearing horrific sounds on the other side of the thin panel. Just before passing out he thought, *I think I peed myself. I hope Mommy doesn't get mad at me. Maybe this is just a nightmare.*

A biblical scholar would describe Troupe/Van Trap as "talking in tongues", making all sorts of noises that vaguely sounded like language as he continued to thrash about room by room. After twenty fruitless minutes he tired, deciding to abandon his search, making his way back to the parlor.

He glumly stuffed his ruined Cashmere coat in the sack, tossing out some of the adult clothing to make room.

The slaughter of two human beings fueled by hate based on their country of origin and religious preference was complete.

If anyone happened to notice him on the short walk back to his car they would see a finely dressed gentleman carrying Christmas presents home to his family. Such a nice man, so thoughtful, putting their needs in front of his, not even bothering to wear an overcoat.

The Doyle household was unnaturally still and tranquil, even the familiar ticking of the clock in the living room silenced, lying broken, another victim of the rampage.

The only sound heard was a church bell pealing in the distance, mournfully announcing the passage of time, tolling eleven times.

Chapter Fourteen

The Third Mother

"What time do you have? I have about 8:30," Colleen asked her husband, shivering outside her sister's home on this chilly Christmas morning. She rang the bell and knocked repeatedly, craning her neck to peer inside the windows saying, "You don't think those stinkers went to Mass without us, do you?"

Mike didn't answer for a moment before responding, "I'm going to take a look around the property, you stay put."

"Okay, but don't take too long. I'm freezing."

Mike walked around to the kitchen and immediately saw something suspicious that caused his heart to sink: the kitchen window was wide open and the lock appeared to be compromised.

He walked back in front of the house and said to Colleen in a serious tone that was unusual from her normally affable husband, "I'm going to try the spare key. Don't move a muscle."

Mike carefully opened the door and peered inside, his worst fears realized, and quickly locked it up again before his wife had a chance to look inside.

"Stay right here, don't let anyone in until I get back. I have to call this in."

"Mike, what is it? Are they alright?"

Mike looked her straight in the eye and made a slight shake of his head. She was a cop's wife, she knew exactly what that meant, words weren't necessary. Her emotions had run the gamut from joy, to annoyance, confusion, and dread in the course of ninety seconds.

In five minutes, which seemed like an eternity, Mike returned with two Boston patrolmen. By now Colleen had prepared herself for the worst with enough adrenaline pumping through her bloodstream to make her feel like she could break down the door.

Officer O'Malley was given the spare key and assigned the job of gatekeeper, no one was to go in or out unless they went through him following standard department protocol, nothing was to be disturbed at the scene before the detectives arrived. O'Malley removed his shoes and stood at the entrance to the doorway looking all business.

Colleen could not contain herself any longer, knowing every minute counts in emergency medicine, time was the razor's edge between life and death. She broke away from her husband and confronted O'Malley. "What's taking so long? There still might be people alive inside? I'm a nurse, I can check for vitals."

O'Malley was an imposing man, having a good sixty pounds and eight inches on Colleen, and used to people backing down to him due to his imposing physique. Pulling out his nightstick and slapping it against his palm for effect he answered,

"The ambulance and coroner are on their way. I know it is taking a while but it's Christmas morning and..."

Colleen had heard and seen enough.

Anecdotal stories abound of women that obtain superhuman strength in certain situations such as lifting a car to free their child. Given the situation she faced, apparently Colleen somehow managed to tap into this enigmatic form of energy.

Grabbing the much larger man by the shoulders, Colleen tossed the startled policeman aside, sending him crashing to the ground, like a charging defensive linemen disposing of a running back trying to block for his quarterback.

As his hat flew off and nightstick clattered against the hardwood floor, O'Malley could only manage a tepid, "What the hell?" knowing the boys at the station would have a field day with this one.

Colleen was locked into full emergency room nurse mode. Seeing the bodies on the floor near the fallen Christmas tree, her mind triaged the situation in seconds. She checked for pulses, none. Rigor mortis setting in, check.

Don't waste time with them now. Maura, dead. Dennis, dead. No Tommy present, maybe he's still alive.

"Tommy? It's your Aunt Colleen. Tommy!" she yelled while ignoring equally loud shouts of "Colleen, please don't touch anything!" and "Colleen where are you?" from Mike.

She blocked out thoughts of her dead twin sister knowing the only way she could possibly help her now was to save her son. She had to be logical, not emotional; there would be time enough for grief when the crisis was over.

She repeated the emergency room mantra in her mind, *Time for tears later. Time for tears later.*

Collecting herself, she thought, *I don't see Tommy, where could he be?* Then, *Of course, hide and seek.*

She bounded up the stairs two at a time, passing over the mess spawned from the prior evening's mayhem, and reached the back of Tommy's closet, breathing heavily, still ignoring voices of authority protesting her presence in the house.

With crushing anticipation, she slid the panel open.

There he was, Tommy in his secret hiding place, the tuck-a-way, curled up in a fetal position, cold as the dead. She efficiently checked him for a carotid pulse, found none, checked again and thought she felt a faint one. This tiniest of "thumps" convinced her he had a chance at survival, and that's all a good emergency room nurse needed.

Locked in, she knew exactly what to do, having assisted in reviving a young boy that had fallen through the ice skating on the Charles River who was in similar condition. She lifted Tommy and brought him into the bathroom. She knew the key to his survival was to raise his body temperature from its hypothermic state, gradually, too fast and it could result in heart arrhythmia leading to a seizure or possibly even a stroke. Normally she would use blankets to warm his core before his arms and legs but felt he was too far gone for that.

She ran the tub with barely lukewarm water, and when filled to a sufficient level she stripped down to her underwear. Clutching Tommy's naked body against her body facing in the same direction with his back against her stomach and the top of his head under her chin, they slipped into the most life sustaining of all God's creations, water.

He was cold. Stone cold. She positioned herself with her back on the floor of the tub, keeping Tommy's head above water while holding his body down from floating upward. She tried her best to keep his arms and legs out of the water, an awkward and exhausting position to maintain, but Colleen knew it was critical Tommy's core be warmed before his extremities. If it helped this young boy to survive, she would try to act the contortionist for as long as she was able.

Five minutes passed, then ten, then fifteen. Her arms and legs began to ache and she was becoming very cold herself but resisted the temptation to add warm water knowing it was crucial Tommy didn't warm too rapidly. She remembered Dr. Siegel's words when a new crop of wet behind the ears interns rotated through the Mass General ER,

"The only real physician is God; always try to work with nature, not against it."

Colleen now heard the many voices that seemed to emanate throughout the house as she tried to slow her breathing and calm down. As she lay in the water, her consciousness reflexively blocked out the horror she had just witnessed.

Her mind drifted to thoughts of her grandmother, of all people, she of the thick Irish brogue and scary tales of the Great Famine. Collen hated her stories of starving mothers clinging to dead children roaming the countryside, she refused to believe them, they just gave her nightmares.

Now, as the fates always bring us full circle, in her arms she had a dying child, a real life nightmare.

We Irish lost enough children, Colleen making a vow to her grandmother, *I'll be damned if I lose this one.*

Tommy's foot twitched. That almost imperceptible sign of life happened at the exact same time Colleen felt an unusual and powerful surge of energy pass through her entire body, just a coincidence when she thought of her grandmother, to be sure.

I know what that feeling was, endorphins, Colleen reasoned, drawing on the logic of her medical knowledge, *it just must have been the endorphins kicking in.*

She finally was able to take a proper breath, knowing Tommy would likely survive, but had no idea how long he had been unconscious. She was well aware lack of oxygen could have resulted in significant brain damage for her nephew, her sister's beloved son.

Lying in the now cool water, after experiencing the excruciating psychological pain of seeing her twin sister lying in a pool of her own blood, followed by the unbridled joy of Tommy's second chance at life, she felt in some odd way that she had just given birth to him.

No matter what physical or mental disabilities he may have incurred, as far as she was concerned, she had become Tommy's third mother, and would rather go to jail than give him up to a foster home.

Colleen cradled Tommy as his heartbeat recovered from weak and thready to strong and steady. Instead of feeling relieved and overcome with grief, she became increasingly angry.

Every day she spent backbreaking hours at work trying to preserve life, be they pawns or kings, no matter what race or religion, it didn't matter, all life was precious. She knew full well even if the scum that committed this heinous crime came into her emergency room, the professionals at Mass General would provide excellent care.

That is, he would get first class treatment on her shift as long as she didn't know his identity. If she recognized him, assuming a man did this, and he came rolling into the ER on a gurney, she would make sure they would roll him back out, this time with a sheet over his head.

If that sick bastard came in on my shift it would be over for him! The first thing I would do is...

Colleen's increasing agitation thankfully was interrupted by a sharp rap on the bathroom door, followed by a decidedly droll male voice,

"Mrs. Flynn, my name is Dan Billings. I am a detective with the Boston Police Department. Can I open the door and ask you a few questions?"

Chapter Fifteen

Dan and Monte

Dan Billings was one-half of the Boston Police Department's best detective team, bar none. Along with his partner Monte Gallo, they represented totally opposite ends of the spectrum of law enforcement personalities and skillsets, which is probably one reason they were so successful in solving so many difficult cases.

Billings could best be described as rough. On a good day he was like coarse sandpaper, on a bad one, which was most of the time, broken glass.

He didn't wear clothes well. He had the type of male physique that could make a suit made by the finest tailor in Boston look like it came off the sale rack at Filenes.

What he did possess was an uncanny ability to read people. He studied their habits, quirks, and secrets, especially their secrets, all elements that made that person who they are. Dan analyzed these traits and looked for anything out of character the suspect may have done to break their normal routine at the time of a murder. Or, if that failed, find another piece of scum to flip on the piece of scum that did the crime.

And it didn't make any difference to him who that person was, it could be his own mother, everyone was a potential suspect. Dan believed anyone given the right circumstances was capable of murder, obviously not having the highest regard for his fellow man.

Then there was his partner, Monte Gallo. Monte's appearance was important to him and he always chose clothes that accentuated his athletic build, Billings never seeming to notice one way or the other but the ladies certainly did.

Monte was a student of forensics, the application of scientific principles to solve crimes, seeing it as an increasingly important tool in criminal investigations. He read everything he could find on the subject and was a disciple of Edmond Locard, the Frenchman credited with creating the first police crime laboratory in the world this past year. He kept lobbying for a similar facility for the Boston Police

Department, but so far no luck.

"Maybe the state cops will get one," he grumbled to Dan. "They get all the good stuff."

Monte had more than a touch of obsessive-compulsive disorder, manifesting itself by his fixation of wanting everything in perfect order and nothing out of place. This trait made him at constant odds with Billings who could care less about such things, but also made him an excellent detective, able to pick up almost imperceptible inconsistencies in the physical world no one else could see.

It could be a tiny fiber, a drop of blood, a fingerprint, a hair, any object out of place, if it didn't belong there it set off a warning bell in his head. He methodically documented every one of his findings in neat block lettering in his notebook that, along with his Colt revolver, was always on his person while on the job.

Billings wrote copious notes in his notebook as well but they were undecipherable for most people, utilizing a shorthand that only he and Monte understood. Dan was more focused on movements that occurred during the crime and jotted down his impressions on who did what to who with a series of sketches with puzzling arrows and symbols.

Monte's meticulous habits and preparation made him an excellent witness on the stand, even wily defense attorneys had trouble tripping him up even when he was rookie.

Unlike ordinary citizens called to take the stand, not only are detectives judged on their ability to solve crimes, they are also evaluated by way of a 'Testimony Review Form' how they present themselves in court. All policemen are evaluated in such a way, the results becoming part of their permanent record and thus their job security, ironically making their appearance on the stand sometimes more stressful than for the person on trial.

'Appearance/Demeanor', 'Responsiveness' and 'Technical Knowledge', are sections on the form that each have numerous subheadings that are often filled in by officers of the court such as assistant district attorneys, one such being the late Dennis Doyle. Doyle had recently given Billings an 'excellent' review and Dan was grateful to him for it.

A typical Testimony Reviewer's comments found in Monte's file might read: 'Detective Gallo was very good on the stand. He did not volunteer info but was very effective when he did because it was technically informative yet delivered in a professional, straightforward manner.'

Billings had very poor reviews when he was a rookie, negative comments such as 'Argumentative, belligerent, volunteered too much information', were replete on his Testimony Review Form, but with some coaching by Monte he became proficient and more professional on the stand.

The detectives often argued about which of their crime-solving approaches was better, even to the point they had a standing five dollar bet as to which technique actually solved the case.

Monte was currently up half a sawbuck.

"Dead men tell no tales and science never lies, unlike snitches. It's all about physical evidence," Monte was heard to say more than once.

Billings would respond, "People have weird habits, but if you can't find the perp based on that, most also can't keep their mouths shut. If you get off your ass and knock on doors, you'll find the answer."

Everyone in the department knew enough not to contaminate a crime scene, having felt Monte's wrath manifesting itself in an epic string of expletives, combinations of words even the most hard-boiled cops never heard before. Gallo was particularly fond of the F word, which he could easily use twelve times in a sentence as a noun, verb or adverb yet somehow say it in such a manner as to not sound offensive to most people. It was a gift.

∞

When Monte shows up and finds out someone got through the gatekeeper and disturbed his crime scene, well... Billings thought.

"Mrs. Flynn, could I come in? Is your nephew in there with you?"

"Just a minute, detective. Yes, he is with me. I have to get dressed."

"That's what I want to tell you, I need your clothes and your nephew's for evidence. Can you leave them on the floor, please?"

"My clothes? Why do you want my clothes? Do you think I had something to do with this? Are you out of your mind, that's my twin sister downstairs."

"Ma'am, until we process everything we have to keep an open mind, everyone is a potential suspect at this point. You were the first one to enter the house, you could have hidden evidence, planted something, moved…"

"Okay, Sherlock, I get it. I'm going to wrap myself and my nephew in bath towels and leave our clothes on the floor, but no peeking, I don't want to be a story you will be telling your buddies about later at the stationhouse. If you want a show, go down to Scully Square and catch one at The Old Howard."

"Mrs. Flynn, I assure you…"

"Save your breath, detective. I'm married to a cop, remember."

As Dan waited outside the bathroom door he could hear Colleen comforting her nephew, and when she mentioned the boy's mother, her voice began to crack with heartfelt anguish. Dan had been involved with his fair share of clever liars that could easily sway a jury, but there are certain unique sounds human beings make when they are truly deeply distressed, and Colleen's tone of voice fit into that category. It was a sound no one could fake as far as Billings was concerned, like a mortally wounded animal, and he immediately crossed her off his list of suspects.

Billings also knew Colleen was on the verge of losing it, and before she could begin to fall further into that black hole of despair, he threw her a lifeline.

"Mrs. Flynn, I do have something important to tell you."

Dan's unexpected statement caught Colleen off guard, momentarily distracting her from thoughts of her twin sister.

What could possibly be considered important compared to what happened downstairs?

"What are you talking about?" she asked, puzzled, annoyed.

"You will be happy to learn I got officer O'Malley to drop the charges against you, you know, for assaulting a police officer."

There it was, gallows humor, sounding sacrilegious to people that don't work in pressure packed life and death jobs like Billings and Colleen did. Cops and emergency room workers used it as a coping mechanism, a survival technique, and both knew it was not a sign of disrespect but the opposite when coming from one of their own, something Colleen understood full well.

She appreciated the gruff detective's gesture, reminding her it was the job of the living to go on.

Time for tears later.

"That's swell of you, detective. You're a real prince," she answered wearily, trying her best to tap into her normally sassy disposition.

Colleen stood up in the tub with Tommy in her arms, momentarily leaning against the wall to catch her balance before stepping onto the cold tile floor. Feeling chilled to her core, she efficiently wrapped her unconscious nephew in two bath towels like a swaddled baby. That left only one for her, which wasn't enough.

"Detective, could I ask you a favor?" a shiver passing through her. "Could you go into my sister's bedroom and get me some of her clothes to wear? Don't get the blue dress in the closet, I'm saving that for..."

"Got it," Dan answered, not giving her an opportunity to picture where Maura would be wearing her blue dress for the last time. "Give me a minute."

Dan knew Monte was going to chew him out royally for all the extra footsteps in his crime scene, but, *She's a cop's wife, after all.*

He returned in a couple minutes with an armful of woman's clothes, reminding her, "Don't forget, keep your clothes and your nephew's separate. And, wear these white socks."

The cotton socks were another one of Monte's inspirations. Made in a specific mill in Fall River, Monte expected everyone working the scene to wear them, including the gatekeeper, easily recognizing their unique fibers under a microscope could immediately rule them out as not suspicious.

Once Colleen was dressed, including the socks, she opened the bathroom door and finally saw Billings face to face.

She gave him a slight nod, saying in a controlled voice,

"Detective, I will be happy to answer any and all questions you might have, but right now I have to get my nephew to Mass General. Could one of the uniforms give us a ride?"

Chapter Sixteen

Survivors

Duncan Troupe woke up Christmas morning refreshed and in an upbeat mood, feeling like someone that had turned in a demanding term paper they had toiled over for months, finally relieved and free. He was vaguely aware of the violence and mayhem he witnessed last night, but that was perpetrated by Van Trap, not him. Duncan knew Van Trap probably would be satisfied with the results of their visit to Commonwealth Avenue, to the point where he wouldn't have to hear *him* pop up in his head at any time day and night.

Troupe became aware his left forearm was pulsating, and upon examining it, discovered a large gash, not a clean cut but more of a gouge.

I wonder how I got that?

Troupe had no idea his Cashmere coat had gotten the worst of it, and determined his arm wouldn't require stiches, just a good cleaning and wrapping. Due to the nature of the jagged wound he was pretty sure it would leave a visible scar.

Duncan began to hum a spirited version of "Silent Night" as he sat down on the couch with the sack in front of him, with a sense of anticipation, just like many children had at this time of year. He interrupted his Christmas carol rendition by saying aloud,

"Let's see what Santa brought me!"

He opened the over-stuffed sack and pulled out his favorite Cashmere coat, mysteriously covered in dried blood, with a torn left sleeve, and said aloud,

"You owe me a new coat, Van Trap," tossing the previously coveted garment aside. Duncan's mood brightened again as he pulled out another item,

"Hey, what do we have here?"

He sorted the contents of the sack placing in one pile children's toys, *I wonder how I ended up with those?* and adult presents in the other. At first Duncan was somewhat disappointed there were many more children's presents than adult's, but then thought he would make a magnanimous gesture and donate them to a local orphanage, 'Not that Catholic one, the other one.'

We in The America Only Party have a social conscience, despite what some people say about us.

The last item in the sack was a box which held twelve white balls with dimples on them, Duncan recognizing them as gutta-percha golf balls.

Hey, those are golf balls! This is a sign; I'm going to take up golf just like a lot of other politicians. We can talk about our plans for Boston at the country club, like gentlemen. What a great Christmas, this one might go down as my all-time favorite.

∞

After the shock of this morning's events, a physically and emotionally exhausted Mike and Colleen wordlessly returned to Cambridge and their residence on Dana Street by 1:30 in the afternoon on this beautiful but chilly Christmas Day.

They lived on the first floor of this Victorian era three-story apartment building they loved for its spacious rooms, kind landlords, and excellent location.

Dana Street intersected two vital thoroughfares, Cambridge Street and Massachusetts Avenue, and was bisected by another one, Broadway. The apartment building was just a short ten-minute walk into Harvard Square, and was proudly owned by Lithuanian immigrants Ignas Vilkas and his wife, Mary.

∞

Ignas Vilkas came to the United States like so many others of different nationalities, as a survivor. Each one came with a story of an oftentimes arduous journey, and this one was his.

Ignas, his father and brother Joseph owned a horse farm in Lithuania that bred, broke and sold Zemaitukas horses, a sturdy breed not much bigger than large ponies, but whose prowess in combat goes back to the Crusades, its strong legs able to support a knight in full armor.

Their small country in Eastern Europe possessed a port on the Baltic that did not freeze up in the winter, making it a constant strategic military target for nearby powers Russia and Prussia. Lithuania was currently enjoying a peaceful period after seemingly endless assaults but, as usual, it would not last.

The Vilkas farm was a very successful business venture, their main customer, the Russian military, buying the coveted horses to stock their Cossack divisions. They lived a good life until the Tsar of Russia decided to invade Lithuania, taking possession of all Lithuanians' land including the Vilkas' horse farm and home, leaving the family with virtually nothing.

But that's not entirely true. Joseph and Ignas did get an invitation, at gunpoint, to become part of the Tsar's cavalry based on their riding skills and knowledge of horses.

The brothers had worked with Russians for years and had got along well but now came to hate them for taking their property, forcing them into the Tsar's army for a twenty-year term, for their cruelty to their fellow Lithuanians and even the mistreatment of their beloved horses.

Joe, the elder brother by four years, was perhaps a bit wiser and wanted nothing to do with being a soldier in the army of a country he despised. He made his mind up quickly, easily crossing the porous border with Prussia and on to his destination, the United States, eventually settling in Cambridge, Massachusetts.

Ignas, only twenty and flush with the optimism of youth, decided to join the Tsar's army figuring it might be an adventure and a way to see the world. It would not take long to realize he made a huge mistake.

Tsar army regulars treated all other non-Russian ethnic soldiers in their unit with disdain, including Ignas, and gave them all the dangerous assignments on the front lines, making them no more than cannon fodder.

Ignas' military obligation began to feel like a prison sentence on death row, and it became clear the chances were slim that he would survive to see his thirties.

After three years of service to the Tsar while tending to the one joy of his life, horses, a drunken Russian soldier shot his gun off next to the paddock causing all the horses to bolt, trampling Ignas. Being badly injured by the animals he loved seemed a particularly cruel twist of fate, but like a lot of life's twists and turns, it turned out to be a blessing in disguise.

Ignas was granted a two-month reprieve to tend to his injuries back home in Lithuania before authorities would come looking for him to serve the remainder of his seventeen years.

Despite broken ribs, being battered, bruised, and suffering facial injuries, he decided not to wait around to heal, instead contacting his older sibling who was now gainfully employed in America. Joseph sent his younger brother sufficient money for passage to the United States, but now there was a major obstacle to overcome as things had changed since Joseph left: the borders between Lithuania and Prussia had been sealed.

Undeterred, Ignas asked around and learned of guards at the Prussian border who could be bribed to make escape possible, that is, if you were willing to take part in their sadistic game.

One guard would turn his back for a cigarette break, allowing this window of time for the escapee to jump across a deep ditch full of water and cross a large expanse of open land. If you could make the leap and were quick enough to make it to the forest and out of sight before he finished his smoke you were free, if not, you were captured and dragged back.

Some people chose to carry possessions that slowed them down, making them more likely to be caught. If they were, their precious items were gleefully divvied up by the Prussian Border Patrol, some even making side bets as to who would make it or not.

If they knew how badly banged up Ignas was they would surely have bet their paycheck against him. But, highly motivated and trusting his brother's stories of opportunities that the United States had to offer to make this ordeal worthwhile, Ignas managed to make his leap and run to freedom.

The act of smoking a cigarette is usually associated with causing a person's death, but in this case, it led to saving a man's life.

Ignas continued his journey to Boston by way of a third-rate ship from Germany and on to Ellis Island with absolutely nothing beyond the prospect of freedom. He came to the United States with physical injuries, no money and the bitter truth that he would never see his sisters and parents again.

When Ignas finally reached Boston there was no celebration, he was just another immigrant wearing a crappy suit, struggling to speak broken English with a funny sounding accent. No one cared how much he struggled to get here, they had stories of their own.

But, the Vilkas brothers were reunited in this fast-paced country of many cultures, all competing for employment, ultimately for survival. Ignas soon knew his brother was right, this was a country that didn't give you a lot of things for free, but gave a you something much more valuable, a chance to start your life over again.

An important fact the two brothers had learned about life: If you get thrown off a horse, it's up to you to get back on again. The horse isn't going to help you.

Ignas' broken ribs healed, he grew a mustache to cover the prominent scar on his upper lip, compliments of a Russian cavalry horse, and got a job at a meat packing plant in cold storage. It was a tough job, but then again, so was he.

The Vilkas brothers met and married Lithuanian girls through the most popular social networking site of their day, the Catholic Church, and Ignas and his wife Mary both worked numerous jobs, she at a shoe factory in Jamaica Plain, while saving as much money as possible. Eventually the couple had enough in the bank to convince a loan officer to take a chance on them by writing a mortgage for this property on Dana Street.

Ignas, who had everything taken away from him and never thought he would obtain property again, not only owned a home, but a fine one at that. Given his history he always appreciated living in the United States and fiercely defended his new country if anyone leveled even minor criticism against it.

The Vilkas apartment house on Dana Street might not be The Breakers in Newport, Rhode Island, but you could never convince Ignas Vilkas of that.

∞

Mike carried Tommy from his car and up the front steps to their apartment where Colleen tucked him into their bed in the master bedroom. Tommy was wearing a johnnie with the words "Mass General

Hospital" on the back, courtesy of the emergency room, those on duty giving him extra special attention with Colleen being one of their own.

The one doctor that Colleen trusted above all others, Dr. Victor Siegel, thankfully was on duty this Christmas morning, not unusual as the staff often wondered if he ever did go home. All the physicians at the esteemed hospital were more than competent, but in this case, as often happens when emotions came into play, she felt he was the best doctor in Boston and wanted only him to examine her nephew.

His prognosis for Tommy confirmed what she thought, physically he was recovering well but it was very unpredictable as to when or if he would regain consciousness, and of course if brain damage had indeed occurred. It was decided Tommy could return home but would need to be hydrated with a tube down his esophagus as well as fed with a liquid diet, care Colleen was certainly capable of providing. Other ER nurses would check in from time to time to give her a break as his recovery could take a long, long time.

As Colleen laid down to take a nap next to her nephew, Mike heard her sobbing for a good half hour before she was able to fall asleep. He took a minute to look at her and Tommy clinging to each other in the bed, looking like survivors of a ship lost at sea to a vicious storm, drifting in their life raft, awaiting rescue.

Mike remembered something his grandfather used to say at times like this when the world made no sense.

This too shall pass.

He walked outside to the common entrance that led to the second and third floors of the apartment building and rang the Vilkas' doorbell.

Ignas met Mike at the door enthusiastically and invited him upstairs, "Merry Christmas! You come upstairs and see our tree, no?" Ignas asked warmly.

Mike came through the doorway and stopped at the landing, not exposing the Vilkas children to what he was about to tell their father, which likely would only serve to take away from their Christmas joy.

"No Ignas, thanks but..." Mike spent the next few minutes sharing the news with his landlord, a man that had witnessed his share of human depravity firsthand, yet somehow managed to retain a positive nature and not give up on his fellow man. Ignas just listened, shaking his head occasionally, placing his hand on Mike's shoulder when he deemed necessary.

Once Mike finished recounting his story, he asked a favor of Ignas and his wife, Mary.

"Oh my God, terrible. Poor Colleen, sweet girl. I so sorry," Ignas said in his thick Lithuanian accent, adding, "Of course we help you. We take off work, okay," shaking Mike's hand.

Mike thanked him and returned to his apartment quietly, not wanting to disturb Tommy and Colleen. Hoping to gain some measure of control of the violent chaos his family was exposed to, trying to make sense of the senseless, he pulled out a piece of paper and started writing down any possible suspects.

He came up with three names, but even those were longshots.

I wonder if Billings and Gallo are having any better luck than me.

∞

"Fuck! Fuck! Fuck! What the fuck, Dan!" Monte screamed in Billing's face, not exactly a cheery greeting of 'Merry Christmas' to his partner when he entered the Doyle residence and was informed of Colleen's barging into the crime scene. Gallo arrived a good hour after Billings, tracked down celebrating Christmas Day peacefully with his sister and her family in the North End.

"Didn't you have a fucking gatekeeper, for fuck's sake? You know the fucking rule, Dan. Fuck!"

"Yeah, it was O'Malley."

"O'Malley? I just saw that big fucking lug by the door. He was here when she came in? How the fuck did she get by that fucking guy?"

"She's the victim's sister and I guess was pretty motivated knowing her nephew was somewhere in the house. She found him hidden in a crawlspace in the attic and half-frozen. If it wasn't for her there would be three victims."

"Well, that's just fucking great. Wait till I give this fucking woman a piece of my fucking mind."

"Monte, there is something you should know about her."

"What the fuck difference does it make who this fucking woman is?"

"She's a cop's wife."

"Oh," Monte responded, now completely changing his demeanor, "Oh, that's different."

The two detectives stopped talking and began to process the crime scene, and would spend all Christmas Day there. Being professionals, Dan and Monte would have left their homes on this holiday and investigated the scene if Dennis Doyle happened to be a defense attorney, but not the entire day, probably more like ten minutes. But Doyle was a prosecuting attorney, which made him more like one of them, and they were more than willing to give this case their full attention.

"What do you say, Monte? Let's come back in the morning. Those people lying on the floor aren't going anywhere," Billings said wearily to his partner.

"Another half hour," Monte answered, not paying any attention to the time, now approaching 11:00 p.m.

"You said that an hour ago," Dan complained halfheartedly, knowing once his partner was focused he was like a bloodhound that would stay on the trail of a mangy raccoon even if a T-bone steak was waved in front of his nose.

Dan's left shoulder was aching pretty good and he could use a shot of whiskey to settle it down. He needed to sit for a minute, and his presence tonight was no longer of much use.

Monte always liked to hit the crime scene when it was as fresh as possible, and years ago felt hamstrung after sundown when he lost valuable sunlight needed to see tiny fibers and hairs. He came up with a solution: a photographer's tripod with a bright light and large magnifying glass attached separately with fully adjustable arms on a gimbal, giving it the look of a contraption, but it functioned brilliantly. He always had it with him in the trunk of his car.

By 11:30, Dan officially called it a night. "We can come back tomorrow morning before the coroner takes the corpses away. Hey, Monte?"

"Okay, I think I have a pretty good start. What?"

"I think looking at this scene I can figure out what happened," Dan purposely egging on his partner, trying to lighten the mood, "We won't need all your fibers and stuff."

"Right, sure Dan," Monte responded testily, overtired, hungry and not in the mood to be ragged on by Dan for his painstaking investigative techniques.

"You can be a real asshole sometimes, you know that, Billings?"

Dan realized he crossed over the line, like he just teased a riled up Rottweiler about to break his chain, but he also knew how to get his partner's mood to improve. This was a good time, just the two detectives alone in a cold house on Christmas after a backbreaking day, for Billings to play that card.

"Speaking of crime scenes, remember that old lady in Mattapan you told me about? How did that case go again?" Dan asked Monte, knowing perfectly well how it played out, but this was his way of throwing his partner a bone, Gallo immediately picking it up and happily gnawing on it.

"I must have told you about it before, right?" Monte asked brightly as Billings just shrugged his shoulders, feigning ignorance.

Dan referenced a case that everyone but Monte was convinced was a suicide, but although he was only a rookie, saw the scene as 'too neat, staged' and deduced it to be a homicide. This case put Gallo on the map in the department and it turned out to be a boon to his career.

It was the fact that the old lady was missing one shoe, lying on her bed with a bag over her head with no signs of forced entry, that bothered Gallo enough to see it as murder instead of suicide, and he worked doggedly to piece enough forensic evidence together to convict her nephew that took out his elderly Aunt for the two dollars in her purse for heroin.

She was missing a shoe, which Monte knew usually indicated a struggle, and he turned out to be right, and the seasoned detectives wrong. From then on Monte saw his job as a way to bring justice and closure to the victim, even if they were some random old lady no one seemed to care about. It didn't matter, he cared.

"I was just busting your balls, Monte. I know that dirt bag would have gotten away with it if it wasn't for you, but sometimes these days I get beat. Do you ever think because of that shootout we got into we used up our share of luck, that maybe we should leave the job and become private dicks, or something? We could start our own agency."

"And spend half our time standing in the shadows, freezing our asses off taking pictures of husbands screwing their girlfriends? No thanks."

"We were lucky we weren't killed, we both lost so much blood. My shoulder still hurts all the time and it's not like we are getting rich doing this. Look what time it is, for Christ sake?"

Monte looked at Dan, then started to pack up. "You and I both know we're lifers on the job. We're really good at what we do and can make a difference. Besides…"

"Besides what?"

"Where else can you work and get to shoot bad guys once in a while and get away with it?"

This set the two detectives laughing as they got their coats, put their shoes back on and closed the door behind them, knowing there were going to be many long days like this one until this crime was solved.

Chapter Seventeen

News

Ellen Davis began her normal morning routine on the day after Christmas, a Tuesday, knowing it was going to be a quiet week at work as many of her coworkers took this week off. She, Hope and Emily enjoyed a peaceful holiday, the family still adjusting to one less person in the household, that being an energetic little boy.

Ellen put on the coffee and braved the cold to retrieve her copy of the *Boston Post,* hoping the newspaper boy managed to toss it in the driveway and not have to fish it out of a snowbank wearing her bathrobe and slippers.

Ah, he hit the driveway for a change.

As was her custom, she unfolded the paper to check out the headline, this one blaring in extra-large type:

Slaughter on Comm Ave

"Wow," she said aloud. "Wow."

Normally she would wait to get inside to begin reading, but the headline was such an attention grabber she braved the frigid temperature and began to skim it right away. By the time she reached the front door her face became ashen and she felt light-headed, and it wasn't due to the wintry cold. She slid the paper under a sofa cushion.

"Good morning, Ellen," Hope said cheerfully as she entered the kitchen. "Where's the paper? It's that paperboy again, isn't it? I'll have to talk to him."

Ellen didn't say a word, just giving her sister a slight nod of recognition. She would not show her sister the paper until Emily was safely off to her friend's house, celebrating their school vacation the week between Christmas and New Year.

When the parent came to pick her up and Emily left, Ellen solemnly handed the newspaper to her sister, but not until the two of them had their coffee in front of them and were sitting at the kitchen table. At first there appeared to be a delayed reaction with Hope, initially showing no emotion, as if she had to read the first paragraph twice before it sank in.

Police reported a gruesome double homicide at one of Boston's most desirable neighborhoods on Commonwealth Avenue that occurred on Christmas Eve. The grisly crime has set off a large-scale investigation within the Boston Police Department as the victims have been identified as Assistant District Attorney Dennis Doyle, age 27, and his wife Maura, age 23.

Boston Police have not offered a motive at this point but…

This is as far into the story Hope could get before getting up, rushing to the bathroom and throwing up violently. She was on her knees for some time, clinging to the porcelain bowl, retching to the point she felt her insides might get turned inside out.

It was as if her body was trying to expel every evil she had been exposed to in her life, but as hard as she had tried to change her life and get past them, they kept dragging her back to the dark side.

Eventually, emotionally and physically drained, she returned to the kitchen and the company of her sister.

"Ellen," Hope asked, barely audible, "I can't read any more. Could you please read it?" After staying silent for a few minutes she took a deep breath and asked, "Did it say anything about Tommy?"

After reading the shocking account Ellen answered,

"No, it mentioned there was a boy involved but nothing about Tommy being killed, which is good, right?"

"I don't know. What have I done? What did we do?"

Waiting until nine o'clock, Ellen made two phone calls, the first to let work know she would not make it in today and the second to Penelope Hinckley to ask to postpone tomorrow's meeting with Hope.

The two sisters sat silently in the kitchen drinking coffee at the same table where they came up with their clever Mary Magdalen plan, the one they thought would be in the best interests of Tommy's future, and theirs.

Now here they were, at the exact place less than a year later, wondering if their scheme inadvertently cost Tommy his life.

∞

A sleep deprived and hung over Judge Gerard O'Neill picked up a newspaper at his usual spot on the way to his office out of habit, realizing too late as he dropped his pennies on the counter he had no intention of actually reading it. He already learned most of the details of his best friend's murder after his conversation with Mike Flynn last night, and he didn't need to read some reporter's sensationalized account of the crime to become more upset than he already was.

Mentally he was preparing himself for the reality of all murder cases: if the police were unable to solve the homicide in the first week, the investigation most likely was going to be a prolonged slow grind that could take months, even years.

Today was a scheduled day off but he felt compelled to do something, even if it was just to organize case files he and Dennis had worked together. Detectives would parse through every one of these documents looking for potential suspects and would be under a lot of pressure to bring them to justice in such a high-profile murder. The double homicide would be on be on every Bostonian's lips this morning and they, the press, and the politicians would be relentless until the perpetrator was caught.

Gerry had lost relatives before but this was the first time he lost a friend, his best friend, and it caused a completely different sense of loss: a relative is more or less obligated to spend time with you, but a friend chooses to.

Even playing golf, which acted as a pressure release valve for him, would never be the same without his sidekick Dennis, and he had no intention to play this season, if ever again.

If being a judge gets too much for me, well, there's always the bottle.

∞

Duncan Troupe normally would be on his way to the Boston Athletic Association at the corner of Boylston and Exeter for his tri-weekly morning workout session around 8:30, but because of his unexplained arm injury he decided to take a fast paced walk instead. When he passed a kiosk and took a casual glance at the newspapers prominently displayed to attract customers, the dramatic *Boston Post* headline stopped him in his tracks and he eagerly bought a copy, feeling a warm rush of anticipation.

Wow, Van Trap, you really did it didn't you?

He ducked into a breakfast joint on Boylston, found a spot in the back and ordered coffee, black, two sugars. He carefully spread the paper in front of him, treating it with reverence like it was an original copy of the Magna Carta.

Well, now the good news: two less Irishmen in Boston, Duncan's own joke causing him to laugh out loud, drawing curious stares. He caught himself before drawing anymore undue attention, taking a sip of his coffee.

Van Trap, you are a man of action, aren't you?

As Duncan continued to read, he found himself titillated, the same sensation he felt when staring at himself in the mirror. He was very pleased with the paper's account until he came to a glaring omission.

I see there was a kid in the house, that explains the toys! I wonder if that kid saw anything. Why didn't the stupid reporter write what happened to the kid? Duncan's mood instantaneously switched from elation to annoyance.

He finished his coffee and picked up copies of *The Boston Globe* and *Record American,* taking them home, devouring every gruesome detail.

Okay, Van Trap, well done, but we have a deal, remember? You took out two Irishmen but I plan to put thousands back in their place through The America Only Party if you can stay quiet. I'll keep these papers and read them to you once in a while, that should keep you happy, right?

∞

Fredrick Troupe's nurse wheeled him into his solarium, where even on this cold December morning the bright sunshine poured through the windows and managed to warm the air enough to make it feel comfortable. His diverse collection of plants had already begun dutifully performing photosynthesis, their diligent efforts allowing his oxygen mask to be removed.

His copy of the *Post* was presented to him along with his coffee, as was his morning routine, but unlike most days that were identical to the previous one, a name mentioned in the scintillating article took him aback.

The victims have been identified as Assistant District Attorney Dennis

Doyle... stopping Fredrick from reading any further.

Wasn't that the same name Stusse mentioned in one of his reports? Didn't he help put my son behind bars?

Fredrick began a coughing spell that caused his nurse to re-enter the solarium to check on his condition, but she was waved away by the increasingly frail head of the Troupe family. After a few minutes his breathing normalized, which for him was halfway between a wheeze and a gurgle.

He was surviving, but for how long?

Could Duncan, his sole heir that was carrying forth the family name have some responsibility in the murder of two people? Fredrick remembered what those so-called mental health experts had warned him about his son, his odd behavior, hearing voices and those pets mysteriously drowning in the pool. Could he possibly be some sort of sociopath?

No, I refuse to go down that road. Duncan is going to proudly carry on the Troupe name with the America Only Party and everyone in Massachusetts will know the Troupe name forever. 'Dennis Doyle', knowing those Irish there're probably five people with the same name living in Boston alone. Everyone knows those Irish breed like rabbits.

Chapter Eighteen

Preliminary Findings

"What the hell time is it, anyway?" groused Dan Billings as he met his partner on the morning after Christmas, who had been waiting impatiently for fifteen minutes, pacing back and forth like a caged panther at the front steps of the Doyle residence.

By the look of it, Dan had slept in his clothes, making him appear even more rumpled than usual, which was quite a feat in itself. Normally he would grab a washed cotton shirt for work, its wrinkles slowly relaxing by mid-day, but today it was apparent even that wasn't going to happen. It didn't help that his partner Monte was always dressed razor sharp.

Their lieutenant used to get on Dan's case many times with, "Billings, you look like a bum. Have you ever heard of an iron?"

Dan would always reply, "Girlfriends don't iron, at least the girls I date don't. They want a ring first." His lieutenant eventually gave up, convincing himself he didn't want to corral Billings too much, it might somehow interfere with his effectiveness as a detective.

"What do we call these, long days or short nights?" Billings yawned, taking a sip of his now lukewarm coffee.

Monte ignored Dan's bellyaching, focusing on what he wanted to accomplish before the two bodies would be reduced to chalk outlines when the coroner showed up around nine.

Gallo would use his fresh set of eyes and full spectrum daylight to search for further clues while Billings studied the position of the bodies. Dan had an uncanny ability to picture in his mind the action that occurred at a crime scene like he was watching a moving picture at the nickelodeon on a Saturday afternoon.

They soon turned their full attention to the corpses, turning them over, examining them closely from every angle, taking pictures, jotting down notes, and Monte put his measuring tape to good use. Both planned to attend the autopsy around 4:00 this afternoon to see if there was anything they might have missed and listen to the coroner's opinions.

The chief medical examiner, Dr. Vincent Marino, had worked hundreds of cases with the detectives, and was very comfortable with them assisting him from time to time. Not that they were crazy about helping, but anything that helped keep their cases moving forward they usually agreed to.

"I spoke to Dr. Marino about the autopsy yesterday, and he said he was shorthanded being Christmas week and all, so..." Monte said casually, trying to soften the news.

"Don't tell me, let me guess. Strings?"

"Strings, yeah. Strings."

'Strings' was an expression used by coroner's office personnel referring to tying off the major blood vessels of the cadaver using large needles and sutures so the blood wouldn't leak out into the body cavity. A clear field can oftentimes be the difference in determining an accurate cause of death, and in this case Dan and Monte would be manning the catgut and hemostats once again.

"How much are we getting paid again?" Dan asked for the thousandth time.

There was one advantage for the detectives at this time of year the average citizen would never think of: the cold temperatures delayed the corpses from decaying and smelling bad. This could not be said for some of the cases they worked in the summer months when they smoked cigars to counteract the stench, but there was one entity that always seemed to become part of their investigation no matter what time of the year.

"I can't believe it, even with these cold temperatures outside," Dan groused, referring to those double-edged swords running the gamut from helpful to completely annoying when dealing with homicides: flies.

Blow flies can sense decomposing flesh from some two miles away and usually arrive in minutes of death. Forensic entomologists can reasonably predict the time of death depending on the lifecycle of the fly feasting on the remains, which is what can make them helpful to investigators, but that was not a factor in this case.

These flies were just what they generally were, a nuisance.

"Hey, Monte, just for the hell of it, check the eyelids with your magnifying glass contraption."

Sure enough, flies had laid eggs along the eyelids of the victims so when they hatched the maggots could easily enter the corpse where the real food was.

A lot of people say, 'I would really love to do CSI work because it's so interesting.' That may be true, but one wonders if they would find it 'interesting' to be in the room when the coroner opens up a body the flies have had access to for days and thousands of maggots are released, cascading down to the cement floor like a wriggling, putrid, disgusting waterfall.

Monte used other unique investigative techniques as well, seeing the value of anthropometry, the study of range of motion of a joint. By taking measurements of the length of different bones of his victims, Gallo could determine if a certain movement the victim may have made during the crime, as surmised by he and Billings, was even possible.

Also, by painstakingly documenting the measurements of all department personnel, Monte could match them up with those of victim's height, leg and arm length and use these policemen and secretaries to put on a reenactment of the murder. The men at the stationhouse hated getting measured by Monte, but the ladies didn't seem to mind.

Every one of the Boston Police personnel played along because these offbeat techniques worked often enough to solve tough cases in the past and the higher ups knew it. As a way of a bonus for their time, Monte usually treated his body doubles to beers afterwards.

As was their custom, the two detectives went back to the station house and their cramped office to write down their preliminary findings, knowing first impressions mattered. Dan stopped for more coffee and sandwiches to stoke up energy and keep their wits sharp.

"Okay, let's see what we agree on first," Monte opening the process, leaning back in a creaky leather chair that had seen better days while sipping his coffee, "Crime of passion?"

"Absolutely, it looked like a hurricane hit the place, someone went totally batty. And a knife was used with gusto like it was personal. It was passion alright."

"Male?"

"I'd bet the house on it. Doyle wasn't any ninety-pound weakling, whoever took him down must be pretty strong."

"There must be a beat cop we can talk to and see if he saw anything suspicious. So you don't think the twin sister is a suspect? You know some women go crazy if they want a kid of their own, we can check out that angle. She busted right into my crime scene, after all and grabbed the kid."

"I ruled her out, I don't think she's the perp based on her reactions and voice patterns."

"Are you getting soft on me, Billings? Alright, for now she is not on our list. Where were we, oh yeah, one killer?"

"One."

"Height?"

"I'd say over six feet based on the position of the wounds on the bodies, but I'm sure you will do your measurements at the reenactment and come pretty close. Again, I'd say he was strong and in decent shape," Dan said self-consciously pulling in his stomach, his body currently not enjoying its former athletic glory.

"Motive, robbery?"

"Well, that one is a little questionable," Dan answered, hedging his bet. "Nothing else seemed to be taken from the house, even her jewelry in the bedroom and money on the dresser which looked undisturbed. Maybe the husband gave his wife an expensive ring or necklace that was under the tree that a store clerk knew about, we can check on that. If it was a lover that was jealous that could explain a lot. It was robbery, but not in the classic sense, something else was going on in the killer's mind."

"The first thing we have to check to see if they were seeing anybody on the side, meaning him, her, or both. I don't think a civil servant like Mr. Doyle could afford jewelry expensive enough to murder him for, unless…"

"Yeah, unless he was into organized crime, gambling or something like that. We need to find out if these two were on the level."

"Right," Monte agreed. "It looks like the perp came through the kitchen window which had no screws in the top latch, like someone had this set up beforehand. Could be an inside job."

"Could be. Okay, let's go over a few things we do know. The husband had a small entry wound from a thin blade that was long enough to reach a major artery. Not much blood outside but I bet we see a major clot when they open him up. I wouldn't be surprised if it was a switch blade, a 10 to 12 incher, good quality, a cheap one would have broken off at the handle. Your countrymen make good ones, right Monte?"

"The best, among other things. It looks like our bad guy was after the Christmas presents, for sure, except for the two he didn't get to. The blood was on top of the wrapping paper of all the others that looked sliced open, probably with the murder weapon, which means the presents were opened before the stabbing. I think the presents were the main objective of the killer and he was opening them when Dad and Mom tried to stop him."

"That's right, and with a kid in the house a lot of those presents under the tree were his, I'm sure, and those seemed to be taken. That seems odd because why would someone go to all this trouble just to steal a kid's toys? And there was the football that was on the other side of the room with no blood on it. Why? Then there's that small pile of adult clothes sliced up and others that weren't that the killer left behind. Again, why? Some of these clothes have blood on them."

"Yeah, some of that blood could have been the perp's, the wife was still clutching that pair of scissors with a good amount of blood and tissue on them. Looks like she took a good sized chunk out of him."

"So let's go over the action again. Mom, Dad and the kid go to sleep on Christmas Eve. The killer waits for the lights to go out, enters the kitchen through the rigged window and starts to slice open the Christmas paper to get the presents, including the kid's. He opens all but two when the parents hear him, dad plays hero, confronts the guy and gets one right in the breadbasket for his trouble. Mom comes charging out with scissors and stabs the bad guy. It looks like our boy grabbed her by the hair, based on her strands with roots intact on the floor, and sliced the right side of her throat in a backhanded motion, probably from the front by the look of the position of her body. If this holds up when we stage the murder, my first impressions are the killer is right handed. The kid heard the commotion and came down the stairs to check it out, probably getting a good look at the guy. The kid runs up to his hiding place, the killer starts to chase him but looks like he slipped on the blood, and knocking over the tree first, buying the kid a little time. The bloody footprints lead upstairs but the guy looks like he took a couple steps back on the landing before looking for the kid again. Maybe one of the victims moaned or something and he looked back to make sure they weren't getting up. He can't find the kid, goes mental and tosses the kid's room. He finally leaves with most of the presents except for the football and some of Dad and Mom's new clothes he tossed on the floor and the two unopened packages. That's how I see it so far. Tell me about your fibers and crap."

"Crap, yeah, right. There was a vial outside the kitchen window that has white powder residue in it, probably coke but we can test it. Long fibers, probably from something the killer was wearing, were found on the bodies and in different parts of the house, but only the places the killer went based on the blood trail. Also, a clump of these fibers were mixed in with blood and tissue on the scissors, meaning Mom not only got a shot in but she may have given us a major clue. You're right, the wife lost a clump of hair in the fight, he must have grabbed her by it. I got some decent prints but they could be from the victims, the killer may have been wearing gloves. I think the fibers might really help us, they kind of look like sheep's wool, but not quite. I'll check them out better when I get home."

Monte had an extensive collection of fibers in the classified evidence room in his basement, part of his own private police crime laboratory. It was so well organized even the curators of Boston's Museum of Fine Art would be impressed with his cataloging skills.

"What did you think of the articles in the papers? The jackals had their day, some cop must have fed them information. We need to keep a lid on those fibers of yours," Dan said, spitting out the word 'jackals' like he had taken a bite of leftovers in the back of his icebox that had gone bad.

"Yeah, but that works both ways with the press. If they get fed enough stories and everyone buys what they are saying, no one will be expecting us to plant a fake one if we want to set a trap. Some of those reporters are okay but you're right, we keep the fibers, and the football, just between us. I'm sure the killer reads the papers, too.

"I get it."

"Okay, let's go through this again. Now, about that football…"

Chapter Nineteen

Arrangements

Mike Flynn sat fidgeting with cap in hand in the opulently appointed antechamber, not quite sure what to make of this meeting he was about to have with one of Boston's most influential people. Apparently this person wanted to add his input into a task Mike already thought was completed.

I'm just a poor Irish kid from Dorchester that ended up being a flatfoot cop in Cambridge. How did I ever end up here on this Wednesday morning?

∞

It all began when the Doyle and Flynn families reached out to Mike to help with the funeral arrangements for Dennis and Maura, and since both families had ties to South Boston, he naturally sought out a church there. The Gate of Heaven Church seemed to be a good fit due to its size, a fair number of people were expected to attend the funeral given all the publicity, and its convenient location on Broadway.

He had an appointment yesterday afternoon with the priest in charge, Father Liam Monaghan, who Mike found very accommodating, and the two men hit it off right away. Father Monaghan's office was a very inviting place, with well-worn comfortable chairs and smiling pictures on the wall of Southie's high school teams, and, of course, its iconic St. Patrick's Day parade.

∞

The first St. Patrick's Day parade in the United States, a modest affair, was held in Boston in 1737 sponsored by the Charitable Irish Society, but it wasn't until the influx of Irish Potato Famine survivors in the 1840's came to Boston that it became a major event. Apparently the prospect of not starving to death prompted these newly arrived citizens to celebrate with a St. Patrick's Day parade we are accustomed to:

march through the streets with a few bands playing the pipes, laugh, and tip a few. It became a point of pride for South Boston.

∞

The two men were able to make a great deal of progress in the first twenty minutes of the meeting when there was a slight lull in the conversation and Father Monaghan felt compelled to take this opportunity as a teachable moment and asked Mike,

"Do you know what happens at a Catholic funeral, Michael?"

Not expecting to be quizzed on Catholic doctrine and never mistaken for the valedictorian of his catechism classes, Mike thought for a minute, searching for an answer. He had been to countless funerals over the years but never gave them much thought, just considering them something he was obligated to attend.

The best Mike had to offer was a question of his own, "They burn incense?"

Father Monaghan laughed, "Yes, they do burn incense during a Requiem Mass. All religions, Christian, Muslim, Jewish just to name a few have funeral rites that actually share many similarities to each other. As a matter of fact, anthropologists have uncovered evidence of funeral rituals Neanderthal man performed some 60,000 years B.C., showing how important they are to the human psyche by comforting families and reconciling grief long before the major religions even existed. They help people to get on with the difficult business of life."

He paused before rephrasing his question.

"I meant specifically, Michael, what does the burning of incense at a Catholic funeral symbolize?

"I'm sorry, Father, I have no idea."

"I was taught the smoke from the incense represents our prayers for the departed rising to heaven. You have to remember how important symbols were to people back in the Middle Ages when people couldn't read or write, and many of these symbols have withstood the test of time. Anything that has been around for over a thousand years has something going for it, don't you agree?"

"I can see that, I guess."

"How about this one: Do you know what the sprinkling of holy water on the casket represents?"

Father Monaghan's questions brought back memories of Sister Mary Agnes, how she tried to get the high-spirited Michael Flynn to pay attention in catechism class, often to no avail, even when utilizing the business end of a ruler.

"The nuns might have mentioned it once or twice but I seem to have drawn a blank," Mike answered. "When we were kids I never really paid attention. We just wanted to get outside as fast as we could and play, but now that you brought it up, I'd like to know, Father?"

"Sprinkling holy water commemorates our baptism. In our faith, funerals are not entirely sad as they represent just the end of our time on earth and the beginning of our new life. Funerals are very powerful events, even the sounds of the prayers and songs and smell of the incense are capable of providing healing to loved ones. If you are interested, I can share more with you."

Over the next hour, the two men discussed a broad range of topics concerning religion in general, the Catholic faith in particular and the meaning behind many of the church's ancient funeral customs.

"There are some special prayers collectively called 'The Prayers of the Dead' that have versions in many religions, and in the Catholic faith they represent the very moment when..."

A knock on the door interrupted the meeting, his secretary popping her head in announcing, "I'm sorry, Father. You told me to remind you when it was 2 o'clock. You have to meet with Sheila Flaherty to discuss the proposed school, at 2:30, remember?"

"Yes, thank you, Miss Rogers. Ah, the school," Father Monaghan sighed. "We better get back to why you came to see me in the first place."

The two men switched from their scholarly discussion of religious symbolism to more mundane matters like the detailed plan for Friday's two funerals, separate ones for Maura and Dennis.

All this philosophical stuff is way over my head. I just hope Colleen gets something out of these funerals, Mike thought as he got up to leave.

Mike might not have known the answers to any of Father Monaghan's questions, but what he did know is that he had to focus on the here and now, that it was squarely up to him to hold it together for his wife and Tommy.

Over the last couple of days Colleen hadn't slept, and barely ate yet still somehow managed to administer to her still unconscious nephew, delicately pushing a feeding tube through his nose into his stomach three times a day. To think the same woman that flattened O'Malley two days ago now hardly had the energy to brush her teeth was alarming to him.

∞

Mike thought all the funeral arrangements were made yesterday, but obviously something transpired last night that caused him to be mysteriously summoned to Cardinal Bernard Walsh's office on this Wednesday morning.

"His Eminence will see you now, Mr. Flynn," the secretary to the head of the Roman Catholic Archdiocese of Boston announced, as she opened a large, ornate oak door revealing a lavishly appointed chamber.

Sister Marie Agnes, wouldn't you like to be in my shoes, meeting with the Cardinal, no less?

There was a wall of numerous photographs of famous Bostonians that immediately caught Mike's eye, like something you might see at a restaurant touting its clientele, which ran the gamut from actors, sports stars, and of course, politicians, in fact, mostly politicians. He also noticed a glass case full of solid gold chalices, some encrusted with jewels that appeared to be rubies and emeralds, and numerous crosses and figurines, like a miniature version of the Vatican treasury.

No wonder they always have a second collection.

Mike could immediately sense the wealth and power that emanated from this office and knew whatever this man wanted from him he was most likely to get. He realized this wasn't just an office, but a trophy room, and his meeting with the Cardinal was going to be entirely different than the one he had yesterday at Gate of Heaven.

Mike approached Cardinal Walsh, positioned on his oversized carved mahogany chair, one that was well proportioned for a church with high vaulted ceilings, its seat a good six inches higher than the one positioned facing it that was meant for him. The Cardinal was a commanding figure elegantly appointed in his iconic scarlet red cassock, with matching biretta making a striking contrast to his full head of snow white hair.

Mike was very glad he had brushed up on Catholic protocol when he called Father Monaghan earlier this morning to let him know about this meeting, saying confidently in respectful tones, "Your Eminence, I am honored to meet you," as he took the Cardinal's hand and gave him the ultimate show of respect, kissing his ring while thinking,

This guy's more a politician than a priest, he's all about power. I'd better watch what I say and play by his rules or else the family will come away with nothing.

"Thank you, Michael. First, let me offer you my condolences for the loss of your sister-in-law and her husband. I am sure your wife and family, as well as the Doyle's, will be very happy with the arrangements the Church has in mind."

"Arrangements?" a puzzled Mike asked. "I thought there would be two funeral Masses, one in the morning and one in the afternoon, at Gate of Heaven, your Eminence. I already worked out the details with Father Monaghan, it is slated for Friday."

"Gate of Heaven is a fine parish, Michael, but this is why I wanted to meet with you in person to explain my dilemma. As you know, the unfortunate untimely deaths of your sister-in-law and brother-in-law have shaken the fine citizens of Boston to their very core, and they are desperately looking to the Church to restore some semblance of order in their lives. That is why I decided it would be best to have one combined Funeral Mass said at a much larger venue, the Cathedral of the Holy Cross, on Washington Street."

"But, Your Eminence, my sister-in-law loved Gate of Heaven in South Boston. She used to say, 'My body is on Comm Ave but my heart's still in Southie and my soul is at the Gate of Heaven.' I have been entrusted by the family to fulfil her wishes."

Cardinal Bernard Walsh sat for a moment in regal pose, collecting his thoughts on how to respond respectfully, striking that balance between listening to the other party's requests while knowing full well they would never be granted.

"I appreciate your problem completely, my son, but you have to understand there are other things at play here and my first, my holy obligation, is to The Mother Church. Do you know the history of The Cathedral of the Holy Cross and its significance to Catholics in

Boston?"

"No, Your Eminence, I'm afraid I don't," a confused Mike said, not expecting such an excellent curve ball thrown by the Cardinal. Priests seemed to enjoy asking him questions.

"I'm sure you're aware of the Know Nothing Party and their attempts to destroy the Catholic religion in Boston, and how they actually held nearly every political office in Massachusetts in 1854 until good prevailed over evil and the Party, thankfully, disbanded. Well, several decades later the Catholic Church here not only survived, but thrived, and work began on building the magnificent Cathedral of the Holy Cross with the help of many of our Irish brethren. Symbolically they chose to erect it in the Back Bay, the former bastion of Anglo Saxon Brahmins. This Cathedral represents the triumph of our beloved Church and the sacrifice of many of our Irish forbears and is not only the largest Catholic Church in Boston but all New England," Cardinal Walsh said with a tone not quite full of fire and brimstone, but worthy of Mike's full attention.

"I suppose..."

"Michael, do you see those people whose photographs are on the wall? Do you recognize any of them? Do you know what *they* represent," the Cardinal's baritone, that had developed over the years to keep communicants attending Mass in a large church from falling asleep, was now directly honed in on Mike, who was trying his best to hold his own, the windows practically beginning to rattle.

"Not really, I mean, I recognize..."

"Those are all people I am personal confessor to, I hold their secrets, I absolve them of their sins, I allay them of their guilt so they can go about their business. To thank us if ever the Church needs a favor I make a call to one of these powerful people and *poof*, it happens. The reality of the situation is every politician in Massachusetts holding office or desiring to hold office in the future wants to attend this funeral, and The Cathedral of the Holy Cross is the only venue large enough to accommodate the number of people I am expecting. There will be a dual funeral, two separate ones would be too inconvenient for people of this importance, and interment will be at St. Michael's Cemetery."

Mike looked over at the pictures, and who else was staring back at him but Honey Fitz with that big grin on his face like he had just won The Irish Sweepstakes. There was also a knowing look in the mayor's eye that seemed to say,

You're in the big leagues now, kid!

Mike knew he had very little leverage, but he owed it to the Doyle's to give it one last try.

"I understand, Your Eminence, I respectfully fully agree with your request. A dual funeral at The Cathedral of the Holy Cross would be beneficial for the city of Boston as well as the family… But…"

This 'but' caught Cardinal Walsh by surprise, sure that this Michael Flynn would have caved in to his every demand, or rephrasing that, every request.

"But what?" the Cardinal barked.

"My sister-in-law and husband loved South Boston, do you think it is possible they can have that be their final resting place?"

Cardinal Bernard Walsh hesitated for a minute, his fingers forming a pyramid, deep in thought.

Eventually he came up with his ruling, answering in his official intonation, "Very well, for your cooperation in this matter I can accommodate you in this regard. Call Father Monaghan and he will give you options for Catholic cemeteries available in South Boston, but don't wait because they might need time to thaw the ground at this time of year. And while you are talking to the good Father, give him the good news."

"What news is that?"

"He has requested numerous times for the church's financial assistance to build a parochial school at Gate of Heaven. Tell him permission has been granted. Oh, by the way, I will be the head communicant at the funeral and will gather the priests with the best voices to celebrate the Mass with me, even that Trappist monk Father Robert if he is available. It will be a grand spectacle, that much I promise the family."

"Thank you, Your Eminence," Mike said, deciding it best to kiss the ring on the way out as well to help seal the deal.

All in all, I think Colleen's family and the Doyle's will be pleased. Not that I had that much choice in the matter, anyway.

Mike exited the room into the empty waiting area, no other visitors were visible and the secretary was not at her desk. As he made his way to the exit, he noticed a door leading to another room, one that was opened halfway. His police curiosity got the best of him and he walked over, opened the door slowly and peeked inside, revealing a much smaller and more sparsely decorated room. One similar feature to the Cardinal's luxurious chamber caught his eye.

It was another wall covered with pictures, this one of photographs of priests, two which he recognized, and both were extremely controversial. One was Father Porter, who was accused by impeccable sources to have perpetrated criminal behavior on numerous occasions, which led not to his excommunication, but reassignment. A nearly identical story was attached to the other priest he knew of as well, which seemed highly coincidental. Policemen are not big on coincidences.

There were so many priests staring back at him with hollow-eyed expressions, looking like so many lost souls faced with eternal damnation even if the Cardinal gave them absolution for their sins through confession, fully aware that some things they did were unforgivable, even with a good act of contrition.

Hmm, that's strange. I wonder…

Just as Mike was trying to process what he had stumbled upon he felt a firm hand on his shoulder, sending a shudder through his body. He quickly turned and found himself face to face and locked eyes with Cardinal Bernard Walsh, no more than eighteen inches away, a very intimidating social distance for most Americans.

The Cardinal initially said volumes to Mike by saying nothing. If he had spoken, Mike thought it would be something of the nature he said many times himself, 'Nothing to see here, move along.'

After an uncomfortable pause, in a paternal, soothing voice, His Eminence broke the tense silence.

"Michael, you left your hat in my office," as he handed Mike his cap with one hand and deftly closed the door with the other.

"I will see you Friday, my son."

On second thought, Sister Mary Agnes, it's just as well you didn't meet the Cardinal. You would've been very disappointed.

∞

At nine o'clock Friday morning there was a gentle knock on the Flynn's apartment door. Mike answered it, still struggling with tying his tie so it would end up being the proper length, not too long, not too short.

"Good morning, Mrs. Vilkas. Thank you again for helping us out today. It means a lot to Colleen and me."

"You welcome, Mike. We happy to be help," Mrs. Vilkas said in a hushed tone. "Speaking help, let me help you your tie." She accomplished in one try what he had not in ten.

Mike had asked Mary and Ignas, *was it Monday, Tuesday,* if they could watch Tommy while he and Colleen attended the funeral. It was Colleen's idea, 'woman's intuition' was all she said when he asked her, "Why them?" Given her state of mind, he wisely didn't prolong the discussion and just left it alone.

Mike had slipped out of the house around 7:00 this morning to make sure he could get his 1910 Model T started up, as the temperatures touched the teens last night. His car, like all gasoline automobiles of his day, was notoriously difficult to start, especially in cold weather. America was still deciding which technology to embrace when it came to automobiles, electric, steam or gasoline, but was leaning toward gasoline because those cars were winning all the races. His car needed a hand crank to get it started, a source of a great deal of broken arms if you don't pull the crank out quick enough once the engine engages. Ask his wife, she'll tell you.

After a fifteen-minute workout, the balky engine reluctantly caught allowing plenty of time to run over to Hathaway Bakery and pick up the pastries one of the bakers made especially for the Flynn family. Normally the company's area of expertise was strictly bread, but because it was on his beat near Porter Square and he was friendly with the owners, they made an exception for his family.

I don't know why, but sweets and funerals always seem to go together.

Mike enjoyed having some time to himself after an emotional week of running around making complicated funeral preparations. He thought about how much his life had changed in the last couple of days since Christmas morning.

I wonder if Colleen and Tommy will ever be close to their old selves? Wait a minute, I just remembered, Dennis gave me that packet of papers about Tommy at Thanksgiving. I wonder what that was all about?

Mike made it back by 8:30, in plenty of time, keeping the engine running just in case it decided not to start up again. Colleen was appropriately wearing a black coat and dress with a matching lace veil thinly disguising her red-rimmed, puffy eyes. Normally a woman that exuded energy even when she was asleep, Mike had never seen her so withdrawn, devoid of life.

Mike exited Dana Street, took a right on Cambridge Street and weaved across town to the Mass Avenue Bridge, also called the Harvard or MIT Bridge depending on your local ties, and on to The Cathedral of the Holy Cross. The whole area was already a beehive of activity from onlookers, to judges and courtroom personnel, friends, family, police and of course, politicians. Lots of politicians.

He noticed Dan Billings out of plain clothes and in uniform directing traffic, no doubt watching for anyone acting suspicious that might show up to admire their work.

Cardinal Walsh was right about one thing, Mike observed, *The Cathedral of the Holy Cross is a lot bigger than the Gate of Heaven, and by the looks of it, even this place might get close to being filled with people. I wonder what they can seat here, sixteen, seventeen-hundred?*

The Flynn's were directed to the front pew on the left side of the massive cathedral and sat quietly as it filled to capacity, to standing room, and then to people being turned away.

The church bell set the somber mood as it pealed in a mournful tone, always set for the lowest pitch by the bell ringer when announcing the serious business of a burial service was taking place.

Mike looked over several times, watching the pews on the right side of the church fill in and could tell who Cardinal Walsh deemed indispensable to the city of Boston by the seating arrangements, with Honey Fitz and his wife in the first row, naturally.

It was easy for him to tell the difference between the politicians and the other public servants, like judges, because the politicians all had nicer suits.

This wake and funeral for Dennis and Maura was a lot different than ones he had attended, put on by his McLaughlin cousins. Those wakes always included a lot of stories of the diseased, oftentimes funny, with songs sung and a flask of fine Irish whisky passed around, and were more a celebration of the life that had occurred, not of a life lost. The essence of the funeral Mass was essentially the same, just celebrated by one local priest trying his best to sing the appropriate songs in Latin with some semblance of classic voice.

He had never given much thought to his own mortality, but being a cop knew every day on the job could be his last and his mind began to drift.

I wonder if I should make some plans with Colleen just in case something...

Mike was brought back into focus when thunderous organ music came up and priests' voices filled every inch of the voluminous space, their timeless chants capturing everyone's unbridled attention.

"Requiem aeternam," Latin for 'eternal rest', the first words of the entrance antiphon giving The Requiem Mass its name were chanted in perfect pitch, reverberating high off the gothic arches. The words sounded as timeless as they were meaningful as the whole congregation rose to their feet.

Cardinal Walsh was right about something else, he picked out priests that really know how to sing. That one must be Father Robert—that man has quite the set of pipes on him.

Chapter Twenty

11:21 a.m.

Linguists tell us there are some 6,000 different languages spoken in the world today that are constantly changing. New words are added while others are dropped, so trying to pick out which is oldest is strictly a matter of opinion. Most agree, however, if you consider the evolution of languages in the context of a "family tree", the main trunk would be a dialect called pre-Indo-European, spoken by the majority of the people in the world some six thousand years ago.

About 3500 BC, the pre-Indo-European language 'trunk' split in two, one branch developing into Indian dialects such as Sanskrit and Hindi and the other branch European languages such as Latin, Italian, French, German, Spanish, and English.

Two languages retained most of the original features of pre-Indo-European, Sanskrit on the Indian branch and Lithuanian on the European. Sanskrit eventually died out, but Lithuanian did not, which is why many linguists consider it among the world's oldest living languages.

Put it this way, chances are very good if one of your relatives from thousands of years ago heard a conversation in Lithuanian today they would probably understand a lot of it.

Sanskrit and Lithuanian share grammar, many words and, surprisingly, even folk songs in common.

In Lithuania there are two types of folk songs, everyday ones called dainos, and others shrouded in mystery called Sutartines. Sutartines are sung almost exclusively by small groups of women passed down by certain families from mother to daughter, and are carefully guarded as they are thought to have mystical qualities, often containing many original pre-Indo-European words, some of the oldest words ever spoken on earth.

Many Lithuanian men were afraid of the power such women possessed, as well they should be.

When Mary decided to leave her native country with her brother for a new life in the United States at the age of seventeen, the only thing of value her mother and grandmother could offer her for her journey was their knowledge of Sutartines.

Mary listened dutifully as they sang them repeatedly the weeks before she left, but never thought she would ever have use for these odd sounding songs, thinking they were based on "old wives' tales", more superstition than fact. She was moving to a modern country with a new language and new ways and would have little use for such old-fashioned ideas.

∞

That was ten years ago, and now here was Mary, a world away from the bucolic farm she grew up on in Lithuania, in an apartment house in Cambridge, Massachusetts in charge of taking care of a young boy in a coma whose parents were brutally murdered. She was babysitting Tommy Doyle while his parents' funerals were taking place on the other side of the Charles River in Boston.

It was about ten o'clock on this Friday morning. Ignas was up in their apartment watching the Vilkas children, when Mary had an epiphany: She would sing Sutartines to Tommy and see if they did possess any powers like she had been led to believe that could possibly cause him to wake up. She still vaguely remembered some of the words, but because she and her husband tried to use English whenever possible, she was losing her native tongue, making her task was more difficult than she thought.

I try. What I have to lose?

Mary, of course, didn't know any highly technical terms such as synesthesia and ideasthesia that linguists attribute to certain words whose sounds can stimulate the brain to produce perception-like experiences. It is quite possible the ancient Lithuanian language expressed through Sutartines might just contain certain pre-Indo-European words that have such qualities.

Mary remembered her grandmother saying these songs were more effective when they had a chance to echo off hard surfaces, so she picked up the lifeless Tommy and gently placed him on the recently renovated kitchen floor directly in front of a new, state-of-the- art gas stove.

It was a surreal scene, the old world in the form of folk songs from an ancient language injected into the new world of modern objects.

It was about ten past ten when she started to sing a Sutartine she remembered best, tentatively at first, searching for a way to produce its unique sound. So far, she wasn't having much luck.

∞

At the same time, at The Cathedral of the Holy Cross, Mike was having trouble just staying awake. This week had been an emotional roller coaster for him and now that the funeral was well underway he felt relaxed, like he had completed his task. It was now up to the priests to lay Dennis and Maura to rest so his wife could hopefully embrace life once again and get back to some semblance of normalcy.

Mike was being exposed to a completely different set of ancient words, these in Latin.

Father Monaghan was right about funerals, they do seem to give people comfort, including me. I don't know a lot of Latin, but the words sound soothing and just right, somehow. I just hope I don't fall asleep and start snoring because if Colleen snaps out of it I'll be the main attraction next.

∞

Mary slowed her breathing and let her mind go blank, and by ten-fifteen was able to recall more of the Sutartine and began to sing it with more conviction, looking for a sign that it was working. Nothing, not yet. There was not one change in Tommy or her surroundings, she may have just as well been singing a children's nursery rhyme.

At ten-eighteen she stopped, regained her concentration and attempted, for a better word, to channel her mother and grandmother to help her with her task.

It was probably just a coincidence, but this time when she attempted to sing, the tone of her voice came out sounding completely different and things did start to change. The molecules in the air became so charged with energy there was now a sound in the room that resonated with an audible "humm…", almost the exact same pitch and tone as a beehive. A very loud beehive.

123

The objects in the kitchen responded by beginning to vibrate in a strange manner, and by ten-twenty, the dishes and glasses were rattling. The water in the teapot on the top of the stove became energized and it started to make a low whistling sound, like it was on a slow boil. The hair on Mary's arm stood on end and she began to perspire profusely but kept her focus, not getting distracted by the commotion around her.

Mary was in full throat at precisely ten twenty-one, completely locked in, and it was at this exact time, coincidently, when the humming sound was the loudest and the objects tremoring the most vigorously, that Tommy Doyle opened his eyes and sat bolt upright.

Mary would always know this was the time because that was when the kitchen clock stopped working, forever reading '10:21'. She kept the frozen timepiece stored away in the basement and would look at it from time to time, like a high school quarterback pulling out a trophy from his glory days.

Immediately, once Mary stopped singing, the objects in the room regained their normal inanimate state and the kitchen became surreally quiet, like the heavy sound of silence after a potent hurricane had passed through.

She would never tell anyone what had happened, it was pointless, they would never understand anyway. It was as if you were a person that experienced an extraordinary paranormal phenomenon, most people would think you either had an overactive imagination or were a crackpot, so you were better off keeping it to yourself.

When you came from a country no one ever heard of, like Mary had, and were just trying to fit in, no use giving strangers something to gossip about.

A bewildered Tommy looked up at this woman with the strange accent he had never seen before and managed to ask in a squeaky voice, "Where am I? Who are you?"

∞

By ten-twenty, Mike was doing a major head bob, ready to nod off. He did manage to sneak a glance at Colleen and noticed she still looked like someone that was still dealing with a thousand-pound weight life had deposited on her shoulders and was crushing her.

If I can just catch a thirty-second catnap I will feel better, Colleen won't even notice in the state she is in. What part are they starting now, 'The Prayers of the Dead'? I remember Father Monaghan said it was important because that's when...

At precisely ten twenty-one, which by sheer coincidence was the same exact time Tommy was awakened by words in Cambridge, words from the Prayers of the Dead said by the priests here in Boston enlivened Colleen in almost as dramatic a fashion. She reached over and grabbed her dozing husband's hand in such a way it sent a shock wave up his arm and raised his body temperature by five degrees.

He was awake now, no doubt about it.

What the...?

A startled Mike looked over at his wife and now saw a woman with newfound life in her blue eyes still thinly shrouded under her black lace veil, and an expression that said, "I know my sister is okay now. It's time to get on with life and you're going to help me, so wake up, buddy."

She must have grabbed a pressure point in my hand, yeah that's it, a pressure point. I don't get it, but Colleen is back alright, that's for sure. Ouch!

∞

"My name is Mrs. Vilkas and I friend of your Aunt Colleen. You hungry?"

Tommy was confused on so many levels, but one thing he knew for sure, he was very hungry and thirsty.

"Yes, please," he squeaked, the feeding tube having irritated his vocal chords.

"I make you hamburger, you like that? My Eddy your age and he love."

Tommy still had no idea where he was or who this woman with the foreign accent could be but the word "hamburger" got his full attention.

Men and boys are not unlike dogs in that they are highly motivated by food.

"Do you have ketchup?"

"Yes, Tommy, of course. Let me help you up."

Tommy noticed when he got up that he was wearing a diaper, and beyond being completely baffled at his situation, now exhibited signs of embarrassment as well.

Mrs. Vilkas, having young boys herself and knowing how prideful they were of such things, picked up on his demeanor right away, and without skipping a beat said,

"First, I find you change clothes, then eat. Okay?"

∞

Colleen felt like a completely different person on the ride home after the funeral. Instead of introspective contemplation, her mind was now racing, dealing with, for the want of a better term, the business of life.

I'm going to have to take an indefinite leave of absence from work to take care of Tommy... My supervisor is going to be none too happy... I have no idea of how to be a mother... Money will be tight but we can use what we saved for the adoption, that will last a little while at least...I wonder if we can even take care of Tommy long term or if he will become a ward of the state... We are going to need a lawyer... I forgot, I am supposed to handle my sister's estate, I am her executrix, even though I really don't even know what that means... I am going to have to clean out my sister's place and take care of any bills she left behind... Can't forget about taxes, they still need to get paid...

While all these obligations and questions were spinning in her head, Mike pulled in front of the apartment house on Dana Street and calmly said,

"You get out here and I'll catch up to you when I find a parking space."

Mike was always methodical and under control, no matter what the situation, to the point where it sometimes drove Colleen crazy, one of those yin and yang marriage things.

She walked up to their first floor apartment only to come running out a minute later just as Mike approached the steps, steadied herself against the bannister, and pronounced almost inaudibly,

"Mike, no one is home. Tommy's gone."

"There has to be some logical explanation. Let's go up to the Vilkas' apartment and see what is going on," Mike answered calmly. He took Colleen's trembling arm to steady her and entered the doorway and the common staircase that led to the Vilkas' apartment on the second floor, and Heinos' on the third.

Not sure if they were going to have to gird themselves for more bad news, Mike knocked on the Vilkas' door like a cop, sharply, with authority.

What seemed like forever, but was more like thirty seconds, Ignas opened the door and, in good spirits said,

"I so sorry we no leave note. Tommy okay, he in kitchen."

Those words in fractured English were the first good news the Flynn's had heard in a week.

Colleen didn't say anything, brushing by both men and down the long hallway that led to the kitchen. Sure enough, there was her nephew Tommy, sitting at a table, eating what appeared to be a hamburger. The scene was so normal it defied logic.

"This hamburger number two for Tommy," Mary announced. "He hungry boy."

Colleen collected herself and sighed a sigh of relief.

"Thank you both for watching over Tommy. I know we're only tenants but you make us feel like family."

"You are family," Mary said, matter-of-factly, "New country, new family."

"Yeah, we got Finns on the third floor, Lithuanians on the second, Irish on the first with Tommy, and we're not sure what nationality he is, making us here on Dana Street a real American family, all mixed up," Mike said before making one of his offbeat analogies.

"We're kind of like hamburger ourselves in this place, mix all the parts together and it comes out pretty good."

It was so typical Mike, borderline inane and at the same time kind of funny, actually coaxing a hint of a smile from his wife.

That big Irishman might not be mistaken for a brain surgeon, but he sure knows how to make me laugh.

Chapter Twenty-One

Rearrangements

"Tommy, it's a nice day. Why don't you take your football and go play in the yard?" Colleen encouraged her son, directing him to the small plot of sparse grass behind the apartment house.

There had been major changes for the Flynn's over the last six months since the untimely deaths of Dennis and Maura, starting when Mike examined the packet of papers Dennis gave him last Thanksgiving concerning Tommy. The documents spelled out a path for Tommy's adoption by the Flynn's should the need arise, which unfortunately it did, that bypassed the morass of red tape and bureaucracy that is normally part of the process.

Dennis had worked for the family court early in his career and became very friendly with its judges and clerks, all fellow Irishmen as luck would have it, and they watched out for each other. Observing firsthand how messy and frustrating the system could be, Dennis picked his colleagues' brains and came up with a plan that would rely less on legal boilerplate and more on personal relationships.

With 'the fix in', the adoption went as smoothly as a politician slipping money in his pocket.

Tommy Davis, who became Tommy Doyle, now was Tommy Flynn, according to the Commonwealth of Massachusetts.

Despite his voice that was still a bit hoarse, Tommy overcame his comatose state very well physically, and was adjusting to his new parents quite well. It probably didn't hurt that Maura and Colleen were identical twins that few people could tell apart, right down to their auburn hair and freckles.

∞

Mary Vilkas was hanging laundry from the back porch when she noticed Tommy by himself as usual, tossing his football in the air sometimes and kicking it others. To her, he seemed lonely.

Finishing her chore, she came back into the kitchen and announced in an authoritative voice, "Eddy!"

Eddy was the third of the Vilkas children. Peter, the oldest, a favorite of the nuns, was already destined to become a priest, and Aquilla, Eddy's older sister, would take a similar path and eventually join the convent. Then there was Eddy.

He was not a troublemaker per se but extremely bright, curious, energetic and a bane to the nuns at his parochial school. If he heard, 'Why can't you be like your brother or sister?' once he heard it a thousand times. All the questions he asked the nuns they couldn't answer could fill a book, a book they would just as soon whack him over the head with just to shut him up.

Being in some form of trouble was not something unfamiliar to Eddy and the tone of his mother's voice warned him he must have done something to upset her but couldn't put his finger on what it was.

Looks like a spanking coming, but this time I don't even know what I did. I wonder if I have time to change into my heavier pair of pants.

"What, Ma?" Eddy asked cautiously, preparing for the worst.

"Eddy, why you not go out back and play with Tommy?"

Eddy knew this was a bridge he was going to have to cross eventually, and although he was not enthused to spend time with the odd kid on the first floor, this situation was still better than corporal punishment which he had experienced his fair share of lately.

"Oh, Ma. He's got that squawky voice and I don't even know him. Besides, I have a ball game later."

"You and baseball. Take Tommy, he play, too."

"Ma, it doesn't work like that. Baseball is a very complicated game with all sorts of rules and it takes a lot of practice to get good at it. He will just get in the way."

"You born knowing to play? How you learn?"

"That's different. For me…"

"Eddy!!" Game over, mom wins every time using that tone.

"Okay, okay, already. The guys are not going to like me babysitting this kid, but I'll do it."

Eddy slowly walked around back of the apartment building and said, "Toss one to me."

Tommy was surprised to have company, already resigned to having to spend a lot of time by himself, and was more than happy to comply. After half a dozen passes back and forth Eddy asked, "You like football?"

"It's alright," Tommy responded in a croupy sounding voice.

No wonder the kid keeps to himself and never talks. He sounds like a seal with a sore throat.

"You know, we're all baseball guys around here. Want to try that?"

Tommy just nodded his head in the affirmative with mixed emotions, not particularly excited about taking up a new sport that would probably make him look klutzy and give the kids something else to tease him about. But happy at the same time to have an opportunity to spend time with another boy his own age.

Neither one would know it at the time, but this simple exchange between two boys would lead to a bond that would make them lifelong best friends.

"Great. Jon Heino on the third floor has an extra mitt. Let's get it for you."

"I just oiled it, so don't wreck it," Jon warned as he handed over his old glove. Tommy and Eddy walked out back again and began to play catch.

The first couple of tosses back and forth were a little rough, but soon the ball somehow began to feel natural in Tommy's hand and the well-worn borrowed glove no more than an extension of his fingers.

Then, it happened. Tommy threw a ball to Eddy that had more than enough zip on it to cause that distinct "Whap" sound of horsehide colliding with cowhide.

"Whoa! Where did that come from? You sure you never played before?"

Tommy was just as surprised as Eddy, but also noticed it felt good, like he finally had control of something in this world that up until now had been totally in charge of him.

"Tell you what. Let's check in with your mom and see if she lets you come to our game. If anybody makes fun of you because of your voice I'm going to let them know they'll have to deal with me."

Tommy smiled and nodded, simply feeling like a young boy whose only care in the world was to catch a ball and hit it with a stick, at last getting a reprieve from constantly having to deal with life's complicated twists and turns.

"And another thing, Tommy. I'm the team catcher, the field general, everything goes through me. So, the first rule of baseball you have to know is…"

The two new friends would talk baseball for the rest of the day, and the next, and the one after that.

Tommy was a natural. He took to the game like a dog to a piece of steak, and never knew why.

∞

It was all Monte's idea, of course, having four of the principles in the Doyle murder case, himself, Dan Billings, Mike Flynn and Judge Gerard O'Neill, get together for a round of golf at Wollaston Golf Club. It was intended to be a way get to know each other and talk about any progress in the investigation, but in reality it was turning out to be as awkward as a blind date.

When men play golf together as a general rule of thumb, they are most comfortable if they play to roughly the same score, kid each other the same way and take the game with the same degree of seriousness, giving this social engagement a high degree of potential failure.

Gerry O'Neill was the last to commit, taking a great deal of persuasion from his wife to accomplish the task. He had been a bear ever since Dennis was killed, and his increased drinking habits made him very short tempered and ornery. Whether Gerry had a good time or not didn't concern her, she was happy to have him out of the house.

The Wollaston club was a challenging tract not necessarily for its length but its hilly layout and sloped greens. Even if you were having a tough day on the links there was one consolation: it had a great view of the city of Boston from the highest point on the course.

Teeing off on the first hole is usually a fairly stressful proposition even with your regular foursome, but with strangers, a man's first thought is, 'Please let me hit a good one so I don't embarrass myself.'

Judge O'Neill was the first to hit as chosen by a tee tossed in the air, pointing at him as it landed on the closely cut grass of the tee box. It was a while since he had swung a club and his first effort showed it.

The judge took a mighty swing at the ball, but it was teed up a little too high, resulting in a shot that popped up in the air and landed with a 'thud' a mere ten yards down the fairway.

The uncomfortable silence was broken with a comment that might be appropriate if they were a regular foursome, not first-timers together.

"Well, there's a real elephant's ass!" offered Dan Billings, with conviction.

O'Neill turned red in the face, thinking the smartass policeman called *him* 'an elephant's ass'. His departed friend Dennis could get away with such ribbing, but the cranky judge didn't even know Billings and didn't appreciate the comment, not one bit.

"What did you call me?" O'Neill bellowed, looking like this foursome was doomed to break up after just one poorly executed shot.

Without skipping a beat Billings replied, "Oh not you, Judge O'Neill, your shot. It was like an 'elephant's ass. You know, high and stinky."

The fuming judge took in this new information and for the first time didn't regret his decision to accept Billings' invitation, switching from irate humiliation to suppressing a laugh in the course of ten seconds. Judge Gerard O'Neill couldn't remember the last time he actually laughed.

"It was, wasn't it? That's a good one, I haven't heard that before. Breakfast ball," he proclaimed, referencing the name given to a mulligan allowed on the first drive of the day. The ice between the men was now definitely broken.

For the rest of the front nine the group experienced a round resembling that of most of the other foursomes out on the course, that is, a healthy mix of decent shots mixed in with some real hacks, resulting in scathing commentary when deemed appropriate.

When they made the turn Monte asked, "Judge O'Neill, we're getting beers. Want one?"

"Sure... on second thought, no thanks, I'm good. And, call me Gerry."

∞

Ellen Davis got up to answer the door, her sister squirreled away in her room reading, which had become more and more her habit of late.

"Good morning, Ellen, is it? My name is Penelope Hinckley and I was wondering if I could speak with your sister," her words clipped, as if she were annoyed.

"Yes, please come in, nice to meet you, I've heard her speak of you many times. I will let my sister know you are here."

Penelope sat impatiently in the parlor only to hear some animated discussion between two women in another part of the house.

I guess I'm not the only one upset at someone in this household.

Several minutes later Hope entered the room and sat across from Penelope who, true to form, didn't mince any words. Penelope's personality had been shaped by her family's history, from well-documented stories handed down from her mother and numerous relatives, that made her understand the fickle nature of life and death and that you don't squander a chance the fates might present you.

Penelope was a direct descendent of John Howland, a member of the original Plymouth colony who experienced a horrible accident followed by an incredible stroke of luck during his eventful Mayflower voyage. A violent storm knocked John Howland off the Mayflower in the middle of the roiling Atlantic, but, against all odds, he was able to grab a rope trailing the ship and was pulled back aboard. He used his new lease on life to full advantage by becoming an accomplished member of the fledgling Plymouth Bay Colony, and at last count had over fifteen thousand descendants now living in the United States.

Penelope considered Hope's education her lifeline and was very upset with her for squandering her opportunity by not latching on to it.

"You know, Hope, you really had me fooled. I bought into your 'I want to better myself by going to college' routine and I stuck my neck way out for you. It's been three months since I've last talked with you and that only happened because I made the effort to come here to see you. I am extremely disappointed in you, a woman with all that potential just throwing it away because the work is difficult. Of course it's difficult, otherwise anybody could do it. You really fooled me."

Hope didn't react strongly to the harsh criticism directed her way, just answered quietly,

"There was a reason."

"A reason? A reason, or an excuse?"

Hope again sat composed for a minute, drew a breath, and went on to explain about her son Tommy and the sudden deaths of his adopted parents. The high profile Doyle murders were still a big topic in Boston, kept in the news because the perpetrator was still at large, and Penelope was well aware of the horrific case.

"Hope, I had no idea," Penelope gasped. "I'm sorry I was so harsh with you. Are you alright?"

"I'll survive."

The two women talked some more, this time with the understanding that Hope's absences from her tutoring sessions were indeed for a reason and not an excuse. Penelope was convinced more than ever the disappointments in life Hope had endured, and continued to endure, like many women of her time, could be greatly reduced if she continued her path to higher education and independence.

"Hope, there are two things I want to tell you, and please listen, because both will have a major impact in your life going forward. One, I highly recommend you reach out to Tommy's new parents to put your mind at ease that he is in a good place, otherwise you could get caught up in wasting all your time and energy worrying needlessly about him. And the second thing I am going to tell you is truly phenomenal. With the contacts I have made, I stuck my neck way out and put my reputation on the line for you, but if you continue with our program I believe I can secure you admission to Simmons College."

∞

Simmons College, in the beautiful Fenway district of Boston, is a small private institution whose undergraduate program has remained exclusively for women since it was founded in 1899 and has an interesting history.

John Simmons left the family farm in Rhode Island to join his brother's tailor shop in Boston to seek a better life in the early 1800's. While working making clothing, he noticed many people wore the same several sizes and came up with a novel concept: instead of making individual sets of clothing for each customer, as was the norm of his trade, he efficiently made up many sets of clothes of these few common sizes ahead of time so when customers came to their store, the clothes were already made up and they didn't have to wait.

John Simmons was thus credited with developing the innovative concept of 'ready-to-wear' clothing, and his idea was wildly successful, so much so that by the end of the Civil War he was the largest manufacturer of clothing in the United States and became one of Boston's largest landholders.

He also observed during his lifetime that if women decided to remain single and did not have access to higher education, they were often relegated to low paying jobs, and upon retirement many lived on the verge of being destitute.

His solution? Upon his death in 1870, he bequeathed his fortune to be used to build a women's college in order to give them an opportunity to acquire an independent livelihood and make enough money in their lifetime to enjoy their retirement and be able to stay in their own home.

It would be called Simmons College, and it was a perfect fit for a bright woman such as Hope Davis.

∞

Hope skillfully parked her Atlas H on Cambridge Street, just around the corner from the Vilkas' apartment building on Dana Street. Although she was technically in the city, she was pleasantly surprised to notice the neighborhood had a suburban feel to it with its many trees.

She stood in front of the door for a second to gather herself before twisting the mechanical doorbell, not knowing if the door was going to be slammed in her face or opened to be invited inside.

Colleen answered, cautiously opening the door halfway as if she were expecting a pushy salesperson, but was surprised to see the stylishly dressed woman in front of her.

Maybe she is a salesperson, some model that started her own beauty products company.

"Can I help you?"

"Yes, my name is Hope Davis and I am Tommy's birthmother. Can I talk to you for a few minutes?"

Colleen was dumbstruck, how many times did she curse the name 'Hope Davis'? If it wasn't for this sorry excuse of a woman, her twin sister Maura would still be alive. Hope's very name made Colleen's stomach turn, and here she was, standing right in front of her. Colleen began to feel that overpowering rush of adrenaline well up in her body that often precedes violent acts, ones that end up filling the waiting room of the Mass General ER on a Saturday night.

I can't believe she has the guts to show up on my doorstep. But, Maura liked her for some reason, so for her sake I won't push her down the stairs. Maybe.

Through gritted teeth Colleen said, "Okay, but just a minute," as she opened the door.

The two women sat across from each other in the parlor with enough tension between them to snap a steel cable. Hope, to her credit, remained composed, as if her angst had already occurred when she decided to come here in the first place, despite the look in Colleen's eyes that said, 'Say the wrong thing and I'm going to break your nose.'

"First of all, I want to give my condolences for your sister and brother-in-law. You have to believe me that if I had any idea such a horrible thing could happen I never would have contacted them in the first place. All I ever wanted was for Tommy to have a good home with a good family," Hope stated quietly but firmly. "Maybe he did after all."

"Maybe? You of all people came here to judge me and my husband? I think you should just leave."

"I will leave, but please hear me out. Your sister did."

This simple phrase caught Colleen off guard enough to change the entire nature of the meeting. Colleen, out of respect for her sister, would put her anger aside long enough to listen what Maura heard regarding this woman. She also remembered the short time her sister had Tommy as her son was some of the happiest of her life.

"Okay, you have five minutes."

Hope didn't waste any time giving her a short version of her life and reason for putting her son up for adoption, even giving a rendition of her Mary Magdalen Adoption Agency caper.

"You were able to pull one over on Sister Apollonia?" Colleen asked incredulously, remembering the intimidating nun that she and her husband had dealt with, like Hope just told her she was able to break into Fort Knox.

Maybe this Hope is for real, after all. My sister was a pretty sharp cookie and she thought she was alright.

"You see, even though something tragic happened, something good came out of it in that you and your husband now have a wonderful son."

Colleen knew this much to be true but still could not shake her visceral dislike for this woman, saying,

"Tommy is off playing baseball and I don't want him to see you if he gets home soon."

"That doesn't surprise me," Hope interjected, knowing she had just pulled off a successful coup in their verbal fencing match.

"What, that I don't want him to see you? He doesn't need any more surprises, he's had enough for a lifetime."

"No, I meant the part about baseball. His father was quite a ballplayer himself, some say one of the best to ever come out of the state of Maine. In fact, he was on a team in Lynn that made hundred dollar bets on a game they won and he used that money to help buy his first factory."

Hope knew she hooked this combative woman with this tidbit about Tommy's father, that she cast the fly and Colleen rose to it like a hungry brookie in the East Branch of the Pemigewasset River in New Hampshire in the early morning. Rare is the woman that wouldn't want to find out everything she could about her child's birthfather.

"That's interesting, the kids say Tommy is a natural and is going to be really good," Colleen's voice suddenly softening.

"Okay, Hope, now that you brought him up, details, I want details. Tell me more about yourself and Tommy's father? Do you want coffee? I can put on a pot. Or do you prefer tea?"

An hour flew by as the two women realized they had very similar personalities and actually became comfortable in each other's company.

As Hope was about to leave, she shared something with Colleen she learned after taking a long, hard look at herself.

"I've had some bad luck with men and blamed them for my troubles, but now I know it's been all my fault. I think it's better if I don't have a man in my life, I just attract the wrong ones."

Colleen would never have thought when she opened the door to this woman and resisted the urge to break this woman's neck, that she could actually end up liking her. An idea popped into Colleen's head, one that she was sure would make Maura laugh and shake her head.

You're not the only woman in this room that can come up with a plan, Hope Davis.

∞

"Is this the craziest thing you have ever seen or what?" exclaimed Phil Lockhart to Herm Pottle as he rushed into their office, like he had just witnessed first-hand something that would lead to the downfall of civilization as we know it,

"I can't believe it. Have people gone nuts?"

Herm, who never takes anything for granted, or too seriously, when it comes to politics, laughed.

"I guess people see him as a protest candidate, they don't like the system."

"I get that, but this guy Troupe goes way beyond that. Last night he called Mayor Fitzgerald 'a corrupt leprechaun'. How about, 'I'm going to send them all back to Dublin so fast their heads will spin.' Can you imagine what would happen if we said anything like that, in this city, loaded with Irishmen? And now he's taking on the Italians, calling them a bunch of 'anarchists and bomb throwers'. The strange thing, the more insulting he gets the more the crowd eats it up, and I'm starting to think this guy can actually win when Honey Fitz goes up for re-election in '14."

"I'm starting to think the same thing. I know up until now the old man has been bankrolling Duncan and he claims he is above using other people's money, but we both know that is a load of crap. We are going to have to arrange for some higher profile speaking engagements to access high rollers to get some real money in the war chest. They will back a winner no matter who it is and this guy is gathering steam. Who would've thunk it?"

Chapter Twenty-two

Developments

"You have to be kidding me!" Dan Billings griped when he walked up to the bunker hard by the green of Wollaston's eighteenth hole and saw his approach shot had buried right next to the lip of the bunker. He and Mike, who already had his ball in his pocket, were four up on Gallo and O'Neill, and all Dan had to do was get his ball up on the green and two putt for the victory.

Up until now it had been a great round for him on a picture perfect New England day in June.

Billings, a study in concentration, was forced to take an awkward stance, one foot in the bunker and one on the fringe of the green. He took a decent looking swipe at the ball but couldn't dislodge it, just causing it to be burrowed even deeper into the sand. He composed himself, took a deep breath, and took another attempt. This he time successfully extricated the ball, but it hit the lip and rolled back, hitting him in the foot. Two stroke penalty, match over.

"God Damn this game, I hate it!" fumed Billings, ever the competitor, while brushing the normally compliant sand off his pants. The other members of the foursome didn't react to his outburst, knowing Dan's tirade would be short-lived and he was always harder on himself than they ever could be, except today they might decide to give him some grief just for the hell of it.

Predictably, he asked, to no one in particular a moment later, "Did any of you guys make a tee time for next Saturday, yet?"

As the men sat down for lunch, the first order of business was always to discuss any new developments in the murder investigation and for the first time, there was absolutely nothing new for Dan to report.

"This case is just like me in that stupid sand trap, stuck," Billings grumbled. "Monte, help me out here."

"Well, the fibers on the scissors have been identified as Cashmere which means the perp either stole or owned a pricey coat," Gallo said on cue, this champion of forensics.

People lie on the stand all the time, but evidence is evidence. You can make book on it, a phrase if Monte didn't say once, he said a hundred times.

Dan was convinced human beings had habits and foibles that were as distinctive as fingerprints, and, like an accomplished poker player, he could always catch them by their 'tells'. Monte obviously had a leg up on Dan with this new fiber evidence and his partner's mood was beginning to sour, again.

"Well, that's something new," said Mike. "Nice work, Monte. How did you come up with that?"

"I contacted Dr. Jon Whisler at the Harvard Natural History Museum and he had some of the fibers on file and they were a perfect match. It was a Cashmere coat, alright."

"Good Monte, good. How about you, Gerry?" Billings asked, pretending to be upbeat after losing money in the match to Monte today and possibly owing him another five bucks unless he was able to locate the perp his way. At least the conversation was turning away from talk of his debacle on the eighteenth hole, firmly putting that mess in the rear view mirror.

"I went through every case file with two interns from Suffolk Law and the only possible hit we had was a person named David Van Trap, but when we went to look for his prison files we came up empty," Gerry O'Neill added.

"Could that happen by accident or on purpose?"

"Both, unfortunately. The record keeping at the courthouse, and The Charles Street Jail, leave much to be desired."

"Okay, at least we have a name. That's progress," Dan said, putting special emphasis on the word 'progress', wishing he had more to add.

"Hey Dan, by the way, I tried calling you last night to tell you about the fibers, but you were out again. What gives?" asked Monte suspiciously, sounding more like a detective than a partner.

"Well, I was going to tell you soon anyway, but there's this girl I am seeing…" he said sheepishly, knowing he was about to get it, both barrels. This day had stated out great until that damned eighteenth hole.

"Woah! Call the *Globe*, stop the presses! Dan Billings has a girlfriend!" Monte laughed. "Does that have anything to do with all those extra details you have been working lately? Can't keep much from a cop, especially your partner."

"Well, she lives in Medford and my car died, so..."

"You need some extra dough for a new ride to see your girlfriend, I get it. Does this girl have a name or do I have to call on my snitches?" Monte asked, tongue in cheek, really enjoying seeing his normally gruff partner squirm like a pimple faced high schooler about to invite a cute girl to the junior prom.

"Angie. Angie Sambuco."

"A nice Italian girl? One of my people? Have you met the parents yet? It's all about Mama, you have to impress Mama. Whatever you do, say how much you love her cooking and if Dad gives you some home-made wine, tell him how great it is even if it tastes like kerosene. My people love food. Food and family," Monte stated, like he was giving his partner the key to his future happiness.

"Speaking of details, I worked an interesting one two nights ago," interjected Mike, Billings relieved to have the subject changed again.

"How so?"

"It was a security detail for this Duncan Troupe, you know, the one with that America Only Party. Boy, does he ever hate us Irish and now he's taking on the Italians, too. I'm surprised I got the job having a last name of Flynn and all, his handlers must have missed that one. Anyway, I thought maybe one of his disciples got all charged up listening to all the hate speech and wanted to take out an Irish Assistant District Attorney."

Dan rubbed his chin for a minute and said, "You know what, Mike? That is a pretty good angle for us to check. Finally, a possible motive. Do you think you can put in a word for me to work one of those rallies, too? Maybe this case isn't as stuck as my ball on eighteen after all."

"Well, your ball did come out... eventually," deadpanned Monte.

"Shaddapp!" his irritated partner barked, like a junkyard dog that had lost track of his bone and knew another one wouldn't be coming his way any time soon.

∞

"What? You want to do what, now?" Duncan Troupe, incredulous and arguing once again with his alter ego, who was making his presence felt more and more lately after a prolonged absence. It was almost like

David Van Trap was jealous of all the attention Duncan was getting lately, and his response was to go into all-out self-destructive mode just to make himself relevant.

You heard me. That kid that saw us, I want to take him out.

"I'm becoming a public figure and easily recognizable. It's ludicrous to think I could do something like that and possibly get away with it."

Ludicrous? Listen to you. Did you learn that fancy word when you were cooling your heels in the Charles Street Jail? Don't try your 'I attended Harvard' bullshit with me, I know exactly who you are and where you have been. People do some amazing things when no one is watching, especially you, and I always have my eyes on you, buddy boy.

Duncan was well aware that the only way to keep Van Trap quiet for a while was to do like the ancient Mayan culture did when they felt it necessary to satisfy the gods, sacrifice a life. He learned this when he was young, when David first made his presence felt and family pets satisfied his urges, but after the Doyle murders, the stakes in his twisted game had been raised substantially.

Duncan felt he already dodged a bullet recently when an ugly incident occurred during his weekly tryst with his favorite call girl, Candace. She worked for Boston's most discreet agency for men seeking female companionship, without strings attached of course, and was carefully chosen for her beauty, and, more importantly, her ability to keep her mouth shut. She had been a favorite of Troupe's for some five months and both parties were satisfied with the business arrangement, that is, until Van Trap became involved.

Normally, Candace would arrive at Troupe's home beautifully dressed and made up, a tempting vision to most men who tend to be visual in nature. She would put on a blindfold as part of their ritual and begin her seductive striptease in front of a full-length mirror before getting completely naked and down on all fours, never saying a word or uttering a sound, completely submissive.

She was Duncan's dream woman, absolutely gorgeous to look at and compliant in every sense of the word.

Candace always assumed Duncan was watching her to get properly stimulated, but the blindfold kept her from seeing what was really going on. Duncan was doing his own striptease in front of the mirror and it was his own reflection that caused him to be aroused, never even once looking at her.

Feeling left out, Van Trap decided to be part of the scene, making this newly formed threesome weird even by Sigmund Freud's standards, someone more than familiar with his fair share of human depravities.

Van Trap had had enough of this banal role playing, he wanted some action and in on the sex, but his way. Just as Duncan was ready to enter the comely Candace, Van Trap violently grabbed the blindfold and pulled it down around her neck, proceeding to violently choke her. The sadistic nature of the act caused Van Trap to climax immediately, leaving Duncan confused and Candace fuming mad. She said more to Troupe in the next minute than she had in the previous five months.

"What the hell was that?" Candace gasped, ripping the blindfold from her throat, totally agitated and in full defensive mode.

"I said right from the beginning, I'll play along with anything you want, but no rough stuff, I don't care who you are," she fumed as she gathered her clothes. "Never call me again and guess what, the agency is going to blackball you. If you want that kind of thing go find a street walker down in Scully Square."

"I'm sorry, Candace, it was an accident, I swear, my hand slipped because you excited me so much. Please don't leave me, I'll make it worth your while," Duncan pleaded to the only woman that seemed to truly understand him.

Candace said nothing, grabbed the cash on the table and slammed the door for emphasis on the way out.

When she left, a disconsolate Duncan asked Van Trap,

"Why did you have to do that? I think I may have loved her."

You jerk, you love yourself, she just happened to be in the room, she might as well have been a piece of furniture. Play ball with me and when you get elected the women will be throwing themselves at you, you'll forget her name quick in a hurry.

Duncan knew one thing for sure at this point, he wanted to get elected more than every hit of heroin he craved for, every woman he pined for, everything he could possibly think of on the face of the earth. He knew Van Trap would be quiet for a little while, flush with endorphins from this latest assault, and he would have to use this time wisely, to make a decision he had put off for a long time.

Duncan went over to his desk and opened the top drawer, pulling out a business card he had been holding for a while now.

It said, 'Christine Daly, Psychotherapist' with a tony address in Brookline. He just stared at it for a minute before weighing his options.

If I make an appointment with her she might help me get rid of Van Trap once and for all, but the press will probably find out about it and my campaign will be over, he thought.

On the other hand, if I listen to Van Trap, some kid is going to die, but David is pretty wily and we probably could get away with it. Hey, kids die every day, what do they call it in war, 'collateral damage'? The America Only Party is at war in a way, a culture war, to keep our country pure.

Troupe thought some more, a good three minutes, much longer than he usually took to make important decisions.

No question, I know the right thing to do, he concluded before ripping the card into tiny pieces and tossing them into the wastebasket.

∞

Ellen Davis was reading on the couch around nine-thirty on this Saturday night in late July, her eyelids heavy, knowing she was about to doze off. It was a warm night, but not too humid, what the meteorologists might call 'seasonal', whatever that means.

Her niece, Emily, had run her ragged at the Franklin Park Zoo late this afternoon and insisted on playing more games until she, too, exhausted her vast energy supply and was fast asleep upstairs. The subject of an ongoing mystery came up again when Emily asked her,

"Auntie, when is Tommy coming home?"

Ellen was becoming convinced the two sisters may have to come up with a better story than 'He's staying with his Uncle in New York' to keep the precocious Emily from grilling them nearly every day.

I wonder how Hope's date is going? Ellen thought as she rested her latest *True Detective* magazine on her chest. *Probably like all her other blind dates: lousy. I know the routine, when she gets home she will be either weepy or angry. Whatever, I know I'll be up for an hour or more talking it out with her. I'll just catch a little catnap...* as she dozed off.

Around ten forty-five, she woke up with the sound of two car doors closing and Ellen could tell the automobile wasn't up to the standards of her sister's taste. Hope always enjoyed fine automobiles. It wasn't a solid *"Clunk"* sound when a well-made car door closed but more of a tinny *"Clink"* of a cheap production model.

Oh, oh… two strikes against you already, buddy, Ellen thought as she began to become fully awake. *I'd better get prepared, I might be up with her for two hours tonight. Maybe I should put on some coffee.*

When Hope didn't come through the front door right away, Ellen's first thought was, *He might be trying to force Hope into sex and she's not interested, like the article I just read, it happens all the time. This is not good.* As she was about to get up and investigate, Hope breezed in.

"I was getting worried, are you alright?" Ellen asked, preparing for a horrible report, one full of drunken gropes and possible torn clothing, in other words, the usual *True Detective* stuff.

"Oh, why would that be? What is it, 11:00 o'clock? It was one of the best dates I ever had in my entire life."

A confused Emily stammered, "When I heard the car door close and you didn't come in right away I assumed the guy was trying to have his way with you, sorry. You must have been disappointed with his car at least, judging by the sound of the door closing, it sounded like a pile of junk to me."

"Frankly, I never even noticed what kind of car he drove, to tell you the truth. Do you know where he took me on our first date? The new Museum of Fine Arts. We had the best time, but I'm a little tired, I'll fill you in more tomorrow."

First date? Who is this guy? Tomorrow? "Wait a minute, Sis. You just can't come sauntering in here after I've been acting the old maid babysitter aunt without giving me some details, here. Do you like this guy, or what? I don't even know his name."

"Well, if you insist. His name is Victor Siegel and he is the doctor in charge of the ER at Mass General. Tommy's new mother set up the date for us, and I have to call her in the morning to thank her."

"Siegel? Does that mean he is Jewish? Don't you think that might pose a problem?"

"Not in the least, why should it?"

"Because his family might be religious and, you know, we weren't brought up with any religion at all. They might frown upon that."

"Yeah, I see your point, the only religion Mom exposed us to had a cork in it. We're kind of jumping the gun here, anyway. We do have another date next Saturday, though."

Hope was pretty tired but complied with her sister's quest for information for the next half hour, like Ellen was giving her the third degree, one that would make even Billings and Gallo take notice. As she got up to head for bed, Hope said,

"Victor is the first man since Tommy's father that I can honestly say I've liked. Good night, Ellen."

Ellen was now fully awake and could easily keep questioning for another hour, but she knew ever since they were young girls, once Hope was ready for bed, she was done. Ellen snuck in one more question,

"Hope, one more thing?"

Hope sighed and patiently asked, "Yes?"

"Does this Victor have a brother?"

Chapter Twenty-Three

What a Difference a Week Makes

"Hey, Romeo, how was your time in the Big Apple?" Detective Colin Macintyre asked Billings as he entered the stationhouse after his weeklong trip to New York with Angie, his first real vacation in years. Dan had wanted to keep it quiet, especially around Macintyre who really knew how to get under his skin, but that was easier said than done, especially since Colin was a damn good detective and secrets were hard to keep around him.

There was a lot of competition among the detective pairings and everyone knew the captain always gave Billings and Gallo the plum assignments, so when the other cops got a chance to knock them down a peg, they jumped on it.

These guys I work with are a pain in the ass, always knowing everyone's business. I think that's why some became cops in the first place so they could sit around and gossip like a bunch of old ladies, Billings mumbled to himself, the good mood he entered the stationhouse with all but gone. For as much of an expert he was at reading people, he bristled like an ornery porcupine that crossed paths with a rambunctious golden retriever when people read him.

"Yeah, we had a great time. Thanks for asking," Dan responded through gritted teeth.

"Oh, and another thing," Macintyre added, knowing his next bit of information would set Billings off, which was generally pretty easy and always a source of great entertainment for anyone within earshot.

"They settled the Doyle murder case. You might want to catch up to your partner. Don't you guys talk?"

Dan was stunned. "How did…"

"Confession, and the Feds are involved to boot. A lot happened while you were canoodling with your girl in a rowboat in Central Park."

What's with this guy, is he spying on me? How did he know?

As Dan was trying to sort through this new information, Monte came into the precinct. Unlike Billings, he wasn't confused at all, just totally pissed off.

No, 'how was your vacation', or 'good to see you back', Monte's first words to his longtime partner after a week apart were,

"Those Feds are total assholes!" before launching into a string of F bomb combinations, some of which even Billings never heard before. The other detectives stared down at their desks pretending to review paperwork, but were on the verge of cracking up.

Once Monte had a chance to vent his spleen, now composed, he asked Dan, "What the hell happened?"

Apparently last week Albert Salvo, sometime petty thief, long-time dirt bag and guest of the State on and off since he was a kid, came in and gave a full confession, which at first wasn't taken too seriously as there were three other confessions on the books already. It is not unusual for crackpots to come out of the woodwork to confess to a high profile crime such as this one, their way of becoming famous in some form of twisted logic. What set the alarm bells off was when Salvo was asked his motive for such a grizzly crime and he answered,

"I am an anarchist working with Luigi Galleani. We want to kill all you capitalist government stooges in fire and blood!"

∞

Anarchists believe in abolishing all forms of government, feeling they are unnecessary, that instead society should be cooperative and joining strictly voluntary. By the mid-19th century a number of anarchists rose to prominence in the United States when its economy switched from mainly agricultural to manufacturing, becoming more capitalistic, and claimed violence was now necessary to subvert the United States government for having a hand in 'oppressing the working man'. Most just gave fiery speeches against the "tyrants", but then there was Luigi Galleani, a man today we would label a terrorist on the scale of Osama Bin Laden.

Galleani amazingly was able enter the United States by way of London in 1901 after being deported from Switzerland, France, and escaping exile in his native Italy for subversive activities against their governments. Once here he attracted attention as a charismatic speaker advocating the policy of revolutionary violence to overthrow our government institutions, that it was perfectly acceptable to kill someone, actually helpful to the cause to get mentioned in the press, the so called "propaganda of the deed."

Carlo Buda, brother to Galleanist bomb-maker Mario, was heard to say of him,

"You heard Galleani speak, and you were ready to shoot the first policeman you saw."

In one of Galleani's publications, *Health Is In You!,* he even disseminated the chemical formula for nitroglycerine which his followers used to blow up numerous "enemies". They created mayhem.

The United States government had a wary eye on Galleani and his followers, who by 1914 were in full swing with mass poisonings and hundreds of bombings of police stations, courthouses and churches, judges and prominent business leaders. Amazingly it took until 1919 before they had seen enough and he was deported back to Italy, but not before many innocent people were killed and others scared out of their wits.

It was a dark period of our history that lasted far too long.

∞

"Listen, I know you guys worked your asses off on this case but it's out of our hands now, the Feds and the State Police have taken it over. The public wants someone to pay not only for the Doyle murders but also to take a dangerous anarchist off the street and wants to know law enforcement is on top of it, keeping their families safe at night. This guy Galleani Salvo talked about has got a lot of rich businessmen spooked, saying they're on his kill list, and we know these well-heeled guys have the Fed's ear. Let's just close the book on this case," Captain Moore said trying to sound convincing while knowing the company line he was giving was bullshit.

"The Staties are in on this now, too?" Billings whined. "I go away for one lousy week and get the rug pulled out from under me. All that work we put in and they're going to hog all the credit. As usual."

"Captain, I know this Salvo weasel, I arrested him myself five years ago," Monte added, remarkably with no swearing, maybe he was sworn out. "I can't see him killing anybody, he's just garden variety scum. Let's see that confession."

Captain Moore pulled out the file and the three of them looked at it line by line. It only took a couple minutes before Billings was convinced it was a fake.

"That confession is almost word for word of what they had in the newspapers, it's a joke. There's one piece that we never told the press about just in case a nut came forward and wanted to take credit: the football. He never mentioned anything about a football knocking over the fireplace tools, which probably woke up the victims. This is total horseshit," Billings giving his opinion, not giving a rat's ass what the Staties and Feds thought.

"This Salvo is a little squirrelly guy and Doyle was decent sized, I don't buy it. And there's that Cashmere coat, a guy like him would never wear anything classy like that, right Dan?"

"Yeah, and he would never buy anything that expensive. He would rather put his money up his arm."

"Well, you two may be right," Captain Moore agreed, "But it doesn't matter, you're off this case. In fact, I was told if you don't comply it could cost you your badges," he said in his official capacity to get it on record, but Dan clearly read his body language that really said,

Find the real guy, but keep it on the lowdown. I can't afford to lose my pension if you guys screw up and get tossed out the door.

∞

Tommy and Eddy's team was on a winning streak ever since they added a new second baseman, Mike Robbins, a week ago. Not only was Mike a strong player and loved the game like they did, he lived on Ellery Street which ran parallel to Dana, and Flynn and Vilkas had been granted permission to take a short cut through his yard.

If there is one thing a young boy loves it's a shortcut, which usually results in the neighbors getting upset and complaining to his parents, but, even with all that to contend with it is usually still worth it. The great thing about this shortcut was Mike's parents were okay with it, the two boys wouldn't even get in trouble this time.

It had been a memorable week for the two buddies alright, a new second baseman, and a great shortcut. Sweet.

∞

"Ow, ow, ow!" Hope yelled out at an inopportune time, right in the middle of an enthusiastic love-making session with Victor. They first consummated their relationship earlier this week and hadn't managed to keep their hands off each other since.

"I'm sorry," Victor said, showing remarkable self-control by gently removing himself from the situation, "Did I hurt you in some way?"

Hope grimaced, "No, leg cramp! Leg cramp! My calf, ouch!"

"I'll be right back," Victor said calmly as he headed to the kitchen, returning with a jar of pickles.

"Is this your idea of a midnight snack?" Hope gasped as she tried massaging her contracted calf muscle, to no avail.

"No, Hope, it's the pickle juice. Nothing treats a leg cramp better than drinking a little pickle juice. It has to do with the electrolytes and vinegar in the juice that are easy for the body to absorb."

It sounded strange to Hope, but Victor was the brightest man she ever met and a doctor, so…

"Okay, down the hatch," Hope said, sounding like her mother before downing her first boilermaker of the night. Remarkably not only did the cramp go away, it happened quickly.

Is there anything this man doesn't know?

As Hope relaxed she curled into Victor, and they just lay there in the darkness, simply enjoying the sounds of each other's breathing. After a while, Victor broke the silence.

"You know, Hope, this has been quite a week for me. I have been blessed to be intimate with the most beautiful and intelligent woman in all of Boston, first of all."

Intelligent! This man, of all people, called me intelligent. Am I dreaming?

"And there is something else I want to share with you. My name has been given as a candidate for Chief of Medicine at Mass General. Not only is it quite an honor, if I get it I will be the first person of the Jewish faith to do so. And there is something else."

"Oh, Victor, I am so proud of you! What difference does it make if you are Jewish or not? Isn't this based strictly on qualifications?"

"Well, it should be, but there is still a great deal of anti-Semitism around, even among highly schooled people like doctors."

"They're crazy, even doctors can be crazy, right? I will never understand how religion can make some people say and do such 'unreligious' things. Oh, what is the other thing you mentioned?"

"If I do get the position, part of my duties will be to solicit donations from wealthy benefactors of the hospital, for new equipment and expansion and such. I have been invited to a very special party where not only hospital board members will be present watching my every move but all the movers and shakers in Boston will be there. I want you to accompany me, it will be like your formal coming-out party like the debutants have, but you are far more beautiful and smarter than they ever could be."

This is it. Finally, a man sees me the way I always wanted to see myself. I've had the looks but that has never made me happy, but being called 'smart' by an intelligent man makes me weak in the knees. Maybe I'll never be called 'whore' again, that word reaches deep inside of me and rips out my very heart and soul. I will complete my studies at Simmons and you will always be as proud of me as I am of you, Victor. Always.

"Oh Victor, I don't know what to say…"

"Then don't say anything," as he reached over and barely brushed her shoulder, causing her to get warm all over.

"And me with pickle breath," Hope laughed lightly.

"I happen to like pickles."

"So do I. Especially Jewish pickles."

They both laughed this time, falling back and getting lost in their lovemaking once again.

Chemistry, you just can't fight it.

∞

I see them coming! This is great, another two-for-one special! David Van Trap expressed gleefully, as Tommy and Eddy walked toward home down Broadway.

"I think this is a big mistake. The kid doesn't remember anything and I'm starting to become famous, someone is bound to recognize me," Duncan Troupe whispered.

Oh, get over yourself, already! And what are you whispering for, the car door is closed, stupid. Remember, say you found a puppy and ask if it's theirs, and make sure you keep the door to the back seat open. Just throw the little shits in when they look and I'll take care of the rest.

Duncan started to sweat, the perspiration making the steering wheel feel slippery as he watched the two boys getting closer in the rear view mirror. He knew this was a bad idea but could not pull himself from Van Trap's formidable grasp on him, as if he was trapped in his gravitational pull like a small planet circling the sun. Maybe someday he could finally rid himself of Van Trap, but today was not that day.

He looked in the mirror again getting ready to get out and open the back door, but this time they were gone.

"I don't see them anymore. They live on Dana, they have to pass the car."

They must have turned down Ellery, you Harvard nitwit! This is great, just great. A perfectly good stiletto and no one to use it on. You're going to have to get me a woman that's into S & M, I'm all pent up, I need a good release. Your life would be pretty boring without me around, eh, Duncan boy?

∞

"Right this way sir, there are still a few seats left," Dan Billings said in the most accommodating tone he could muster, being in the foulest of moods since he was dismissed from the Doyle murder case. It had been a totally lousy week for Dan after he came back from a great week in New York, and Angie knew enough to give him space, knowing he would let it go eventually.

Yeah, right.

Not only was he not happy at work these days, this moonlighting job working security for this America Only Party rally made him feel like a total sellout, even though it was nice of Mike to set him up to make a few extra bucks.

It's amazing what guys will do when the end result helps them get laid.

Dan scanned the crowd as good cops do, not really caring if something happened to the idiots assembled here, just more out of habit than anything else. The head idiot was about to hit the stage as wild applause filled the hall, patriotic music playing and American flags fervently waving.

All this racket just managed to give Billings the first inkling a headache was coming on, and it was going to be a beauty.

He looked around again and caught a glimpse of something that sent a shot of adrenaline right up his spine, his headache suddenly gone. Not easily surprised by any one of his fellow man he considered capable of anything, what he just witnessed stunned him.

What the... You have to be shitting me!

The crowd hit fever pitch as Dan's week suddenly improved.

Chapter Twenty-Four

Eighty Percent

"Just how sure are you?"

"About eighty percent, but the other one is nice, too. Tell you what, why don't we call Mom and have her come in to give her opinion?"

Hope just gave her sister a withering look with that suggestion, her patience starting to wear thin after trying to pick out the perfect dress in the Jordan Marsh women's department all morning.

Ellen was referring to their mother, Delores, dispensing her version of fashion sense to them when they were ten and twelve respectively.

"You know girls, its simple when you are shopping for a dress. When in doubt, pick the one that shows off your cleavage the best. Men are suckers for that, get it? Suckers?" as she guffawed heartily at her own double entendre joke, whose punchline her daughters wouldn't get until years later.

"Right. Maybe I should just get both of them."

"You know Hope, I have never seen you so man crazy before, don't you think you are worrying a little too much about this party you are going to? Any man would give his eye teeth to have you on their arm, in fact, *all* the ladies and the men will notice you. What's the problem?" Ellen asked testily.

"I told you, this is not about me, it's about Victor. The last thing in the world I want is to cause him any embarrassment or the slightest bit of gossip. If I did I swear I would never forgive myself. This party represents to me way more than you could possibly understand, my whole future and Victor's is riding on it. Is there something you're upset about, something you're not saying?"

Ellen kept quiet for a minute before deciding to unload to her sister and best friend.

"Well, yes, Hope, there is. I feel like I am getting kicked to the curb here. Ever since we've been little girls it's just been me and you, through thick and thin, like we're a team or something. Now this guy Victor comes into your life, and, don't get me wrong, I'm happy for you, but I see my future and it looks lonely. No you, no Emily, just me and a bunch of crappy magazines on a Saturday night. I wish I could be brave like you and take a chance with meeting men, but I can't. I just can't," Ellen said, as her eyes started to tear up.

"Hold on here, you're jumping the gun, Sis. With everything else going on, I didn't have a chance to really talk to you. First of all, Victor shared with me something about his past that he keeps secret."

"Oh?" Ellen responded, her tears now replaced with curiosity, sure her sister would tell her something about her boyfriend that rivaled something in *True Detective*.

"I read about people like him. He's one of those serial killers, right? He's a doctor and knows about all kind of drugs to take out people he doesn't like."

Hope just stared at her sister for a minute, she of the overactive imagination.

"No, of course not, it's nothing like that. He told me he was married very young with a daughter when he was going to medical school, but both his wife and child died in a gas explosion at their apartment complex. He was devastated but somehow managed to muster the strength to finish his studies, and now look where he is. He said something to me, 'Once you climb out of a dark hole it's easier to just keep climbing', something like that. Please never let him know I told you."

"Hope, I'm sorry, I had no idea."

"How could you. The important thing for you to know is the two of us have talked about our possible future together, and he brought this up, not me, that he wants to include you and Emily into our household if we get married someday. That's one of the reasons this event is so important to the both of us, and you, if it goes as planned. If not, well, I'd rather not think about it."

"He wants to include me? What is this guy, some kind of a saint?"

Hope laughed, "No, he's no saint but he is one of the most positive people I have ever met. He tries to make the best of every situation and I can't get enough of him."

"He really said that about me? That's a horse of a different color now, isn't it? In that case, take the blue one, that shows off *less* cleavage, sorry, Mom. And another thing, let me do your makeup when the time comes, it has to be just right, like you don't have any on. I can fix that blemish and no one will notice."

"Blemish? I have a blemish? No one ever told me that."

"That's because they're not your sister, I am. That's what sisters do."

"Okay, thanks, I think. Ellen, I did mention Isabella Stuart Gardner is hosting this party in the Parker House ballroom, didn't I?"

"Let me think," Ellen responded brightly while placing her index finger against her temple, "I would say, 'Yes'. You only told me fifty times, already."

∞

The city of Boston is not generally known for its flamboyant characters as say a city such as San Francisco, for instance, but Isabella Stuart Gardner definitely fit into that category and then some. She was just one of those rare people that made life seem like more fun when you were in her presence, living her life with zest as she became one of America's greatest patrons of artists and collectors of art in the late 1800s and early 1900s. She would eventually establish The Isabella Stewart Gardner Museum, which was her home, modeled after a Renaissance palace in Venice. This is the very same museum that would be the site of America's largest art heist in history, still unsolved at the time of this writing.

Isabella managed to fill gossip columns with her reputation for style, far outside the norm of the day, and her sometimes unconventional behavior. Besides her love of the arts, she was also one of Boston's most diehard Red Sox fans, often attending games in her signature plumed hat, her noteworthy presence appreciated by the players and fans, with the exception of the ones sitting directly behind her, of course.

To illustrate how buttoned down and staid Boston was in her day, Isabella almost caused a riot at a surprise appearance at the very formal Boston Symphony Orchestra in 1912, which happened to be the year 'The Old Towne Team' won the World Series, when she wore a head band with the words, "Oh, you Red Sox" written on it.

The town went into a frenzy, a reaction like someone today posting a video of someone twerking with the Pope, but even that probably wouldn't raise the ruckus Isabella did.

∞

If there ever were a fund raiser for Massachusetts General Hospital in 1912, who better to host it than the flamboyant Isabella Stuart Gardner, who was constantly surrounded by some of the more affluent Bostonians, and what better place than the ballroom of the spectacular Parker House Hotel.

The decision by the board of directors to choose her for this honor was far from unanimous, in fact, eighty percent were against it, the president of the hospital in one of his last official acts choosing to override them. Dissenters that planned on attending the event would be keeping an eye on the proceedings, half hoping Mrs. Gardner would do something scandalous to make their vote against her appear correct, and "that doctor", the outgoing president recommended for chief of surgery, look like the fool.

The ones that approved of Isabella wouldn't mind something controversial happening as well, just for general entertainment purposes and to generate press for the cause.

Either way, with so much riding on the outcome, contentious board members also knew their high profile positions might be in jeopardy, depending on the outcome of the fundraiser, putting many people on edge at Parker House Hotel.

Mrs. Gardner graciously agreed to host the event, a cause she firmly believed in by the way, but with two stipulations: Number one, the theme would be strictly her choosing, and two, it would be a complete surprise. The savvy Isabella knew this would get people talking and would 'Make this fundraiser for Mass General Hospital the place to be for the who's-who of Boston.'

She was also well aware she would have a much better chance of prying money out of those fat wallets if she were able to get people attending to say the next morning, "You'll never guess where I was last night!"

∞

"How sure are you about this, Dan?" asked Gerry O'Neill, using his official judge's voice and demeanor, well aware the subject matter being discussed could drastically change careers, and lives, forever. Dan thought he figured out who murdered Dennis and Maura Doyle, but there was still room for doubt.

"About eighty percent."

"Well, I'm sorry to say that's not good enough, a good defense attorney can feast off of twenty percent, all they need do is cast a shadow of a doubt in one juror's mind. Good luck," he said by way of saying goodbye, but it somehow sounded more like an ominous warning to Dan, Monte and Mike. Life sure seemed simpler when the four of them just tried to solve the greens at Wollaston, not the Doyle murder case.

Mike was the odd man out, he being a Cambridge cop and the only one married with a kid at home. If he went along with Dan and Monte and this thing blew up in their faces, he knew he would probably lose his badge, so he had a lot to think about. Tommy was doing so well at baseball with his best friend Eddy, and Colleen loved living on Dana Street with the Vilkas' upstairs, but they would most likely have to move from Cambridge if he still wanted to work as a policeman somewhere.

I've got a lot to lose, here. Probably much more than they do.

The three men sat there for a minute thinking before Monte spoke up.

"Mike, did I ever tell you about the shootout Dan and I got into and what that asshole sitting across from you did?"

"Monte, no use bringing up…"

"Shut the fuck up, I'm fucking talking here!" Monte accentuating his statement by flashing his middle finger in his partner's face for good measure.

"Like I was saying, Dan and I were closing in on this worm that was responsible for a string of robberies in the North End. We entered his place on Prince Street, I went in first and before I knew it, *Bam!*, the fucker shot me in the gut on my right side. I went down hard, bleeding all over the place and lost my gun for good measure. I was a dead duck, starting to pass out, and the perp had a clear shot at me to finish me off. Then this Irish bastard partner of mine moved real quick and jumped on top of me, taking the next bullet meant for me in the shoulder, the fucking idiot. Dan not only got off a couple of shots and took the asshole out, he dragged his own sorry ass out on the street and got us help before passing out himself. We both almost died from losing so much blood, but there was some young Jewish doctor at the

Mass General, I forget his name, that wouldn't give up on us long after his shift was over. So, here we are."

"Monte might be exaggerating a little…"

"Didn't I tell you to shut the fuck up?" Monte asked Billings with his voice raised, but not with anger, more like affection, as only a cop could to his partner that he was absolutely sure always had his back when things went South. It was a bond cops have the general public could never, ever understand.

"So Mike, you do what you have to do, but I'm with Billings on this one. I'm just going to let the fucking chips fall as they fucking may."

Mike, hearing this story in full for the first time had his mind made up, not hesitating for even five seconds.

"Me, too. Count me in."

∞

"Do you realize who is going to be attending this event? Only all the big rollers in town, that's who. I can't believe it!" enthused Herm Pottle to his cohort, Phil Lockhart.

"I guess if you hang around this world long enough you see just about everything, right, Phil?"

"That's for sure Herm, that's for sure. The thing is, depending how our boy does with all those overstuffed wallets, are you thinking what I'm thinking?"

"You mean, Duncan Troupe for governor someday?"

"Hey, with enough money behind him you just never know, this guy could even run for president if that happened. Let's face it, Herm, this is one beautiful country we are living in!"

"Yeah, it's full of real beauts, alright. We ought to know, we're backing one! And guess what, he might actually win!"

This set the two men to laughing so hard Herm had trouble catching his breath, reality always being crazier than anything a person could make up.

Chapter Twenty-Five
One Hell of a Night

"Are you a Davis from Marblehead, dear?" Mrs. Edythe Smyth grilled Hope, searching for a thread to braid a rope, with the intention of hanging her with it.

Mrs. Smyth was a longtime board member for Mass General and she was not a happy woman these days: not happy with the flamboyant Isabella Stuart Garner as chairperson for this, in her opinion, overly ostentatious event; not happy with the out-going president for over-riding her vote, and certainly not happy with the heritage of the doctor recommended to become Chief of Medicine, who happened to be standing just to the right of her.

Hope felt a shudder of debilitating nervousness overtake her senses, the first sign of one of her dreaded panic attacks, feeling completely overmatched on just her first conversation of the evening.

What was I thinking? I was a fool to think I could overcome my past. This is turning into a disaster.

"I..." Hope began to stammer and was sinking fast, that is, until Victor calmly cut right in, like he was intubating a critical patient in the ER.

"No, Edythe, but you should know *this* Miss Davis is a protégé of Penelope Hinckley, and she is two semesters away from graduating with honors from Simmons College."

This time it was Edythe's turn to feel uncomfortable due to her own history, that despite her best efforts, she had to drop out of Wellesley after three semesters when she could no longer handle the curriculum. It was a source of embarrassment and shame for her that she never discussed and she suddenly wanted this topic to end quickly.

"That's very admirable, Miss Davis. I know Penelope quite well and for her to back you says volumes. Oh, it has been a pleasure to meet you but I must run. I see Nina Meyer standing by herself and in the need of company," as Edythe slipped away, Hope passing her first test of the evening.

"Thank you, Victor, I just froze. How did you..."

"Hey, don't forget what I do for a living, you have to be able to think on your feet quickly. That should keep the old battle-axe off your back for a while, just relax and enjoy every minute of the party from now on. Isabella really pulled out all the stops tonight, didn't she? Aren't you glad we got a heads-up on her theme?"

Isabella Stuart Gardner had transformed the already impressive ballroom of The Parker House Hotel into showcasing tonight's theme, that being 'opposites', much of the decorating having been assembled by art students. Unfortunately, one fell from scaffolding and broke his leg a week ago, requiring a trip to the Mass General ER when Victor happened to be manning the floor. ER doctors always ask, "What happened?" trying to get a sense if violence was involved and a call to the police was necessary, but in this case the injured student just nervously babbled on for ten minutes, spilling the beans on Isabella's well-guarded secret.

After disclosing this nugget to Hope, the couple decided to take a chance and reconsider their wardrobes for this event, Hope visiting Jordan Marsh *again,* this time returning with a striking white dress complete with matching fascinator replete with a white feather to pay homage to the hostess.

Victor wore a black tuxedo, which many men tonight did, but stood out with a black shirt and tie, completing the eye-catching couple's statement with their own version of 'opposites', 'black and white', dressed in such a manner they appeared to be 'in-the-know'.

Hope was blessed with well-documented, classic beauty, but it was Victor's appearance cutting a fine figure tonight that caught people's eye. Never once having been mistaken for a movie star, Victor always possessed a charismatic, energetic attractiveness about him, and it didn't hurt that he was in excellent shape, his physique making him stand out in the crowd this evening.

Most men attending such fundraisers as this that had accumulated the kind of money the hospital was trying to tap were much older and had chosen to spend countless hours at work seeking fortune while neglecting their health. Many were just too tired at the end of the day, fighting battles in the world of business, to even think about working out at a gym or even taking a spirited walk, and tended to be over-weight and stooped over.

Dr. Victor Siegel, when he wasn't saving lives and limbs at one of the country's best hospitals, had among his numerous interests a passion for hockey, and was actually considered a decent defenseman by the players in his men's league, giving him an opportunity to get plenty of vigorous exercise. Who knew?

Isabella had assembled a quintet made up of an eclectic mix of some of Boston's finest musicians, including ... is that a nun in full habit playing violin? It was, and as she stood to play a solo version of Vivaldi's *Spring*, Isabella made her grand entrance, a subtle 'opposite' of the hostess, as it was well into the fall season.

Hope looked up and got her second jolt of the night.

What? Could that be? It is, that's Sister Apollonia! I can't let her see me, she might recognize me and if people hear us talking they could get a good dose of gossip to use against me and ultimately Victor. I have to stay away from that part of the room.

As Hope got nervous again, Isabella strode to the podium and announced to the rapt audience, all abuzz,

"Good evening everyone," the large feather in her hat moving in a manner that seemed to accentuate her words.

"I promised the board of directors of Massachusetts General Hospital an interesting evening and I expect not only this to be true but hope you will show your appreciation by your vital donations for such a worthy cause," to a smattering of applause.

"The theme of the evening if you haven't figured out by now is 'opposites', and there are many examples about the room created by students of our wonderful Massachusetts College of Art. You will find under the centerpiece of your table a scorecard of sorts for a contest you may participate in if you so choose. If you can list as many opposite pairs you see and write them down, I will choose the winning table based on what I determine to be the most correct answers. What are you playing for? The table with the most correct answers will be my guests for an elegant five course dinner in the courtyard of my home."

The appreciative audience stood and clapped, most very happy to participate in such a clever hunt, this evening promising to be something far different than the usual predictable fundraisers they attended, that is, fun.

Victor was assigned team captain at his and Hope's table and immediately wrote their names on the paper with 'black and white' along with the centerpiece that consisted of two arrows representing 'up and down'. They had also noted some of the unusual decorations in the room, large depictions of flames reaching from the floor to a conical point that were directly under a similar shape that looked like an icicle.

"I get it, they are two opposites: 'stalactites and stalagmites' and 'fire and ice'. Clever, very clever," Victor laughed, getting into the spirit Isabella intended.

"I see a full length mirror near the podium, let's see what that's about."

The mirror was too close to the all-knowing Sister Apollonia for Hope to be comfortable, choosing to avoid being anywhere near her just to be on the safe side.

"Victor, you go, I need a glass of water. I'll catch up," Hope said as Victor trooped off with the rest of people from their table, everyone energized by Isabella's challenge.

Whew! That's enough surprises for one night, Hope thought. But no, the fates weren't done with her yet, not by a long shot.

She glanced across the room and got an even bigger shock on what was turning out to be an evening she would never forget.

It caused her to flash back to the last morning they saw each other years ago, the confusion, the miscommunication, the disappointment. It was Tommy's father she saw across the room, looking hale and dapper as usual, accompanied by an unusually tall woman who not only served to accentuate his short stature but inadvertently made the couple an unintended entry in the opposites contest.

Hope was immediately flooded with mixed emotions.

I would love to tell him about Simmons College, he would be so proud of me… about my new life… to thank him for everything he did for me… to tell him he has a son, a great boy that loves baseball, just like him… but, it's not in the cards…

He began to take several steps toward Hope, something she had dreamt about often before Victor came into her life, but everything was different now, her priorities had changed. Hope's heart skipped a beat as she subtly shook her head, immediately stopping his advance.

He smiled, seeming to understand, tipped his top hat, and disappeared into the crowd and out of her life once again.

This night! I feel like the room is closing in on me, that I can hardly breathe. I have to keep my composure for Victor, but it feels like all the sins of my past are being thrown in my face, mocking me for thinking I had the nerve to deserve a better life.

Her self-deprecating, defeatist mood lightened slightly when Victor returned.

"I'm not sure what Isabella had in mind with that mirror but we wrote 'won' on a piece of paper and in the reflection it looked like 'now'. That's probably it, words come out opposite in a mirror."

But the mirror wasn't part of Isabella's doing at all. It had been placed there by Dan Billings, the tenacious detective that was searching for that elusive 'twenty percent' to make his case against his main suspect in the Doyle murders airtight. Dan knew he was rolling the dice here, that if his plan backfired he would not only kill his own career, but would also take down those of Monte, Mike and even O'Malley.

I wish I had a better look at the guy's actions last time, but still, I'm almost positive he's the murderer by his movements. Like O'Neill said though, 'almost' will get me hung and him off Scot free by some asshole defense lawyer.

Dan and Mike were at the function in the official capacity of security detail, but Monte and O'Malley were also there, but undercover, each working a food station. If Billings wasn't so stressed he would be getting a kick out of seeing Monte dressed as a waiter, but as it was it would be a miracle if Dan didn't clench his teeth so hard and break a cusp off from of one of his remaining molars.

Hope stayed very close to the security of her table while Victor confidently made the rounds about the room, and she noticed how well received he was.

If I can just manage to not draw any more attention to myself, they should approve Victor without a problem. Two more hours, I can do this.

As Hope relaxed a bit, enough to draw a decent breath once again, Isabella commanded the podium once more.

"Ladies and gentlemen, in the spirit of our theme tonight, I have invited two candidates running for mayor of our city of Boston that are polar opposites politically and philosophically to give us their best stump speech. One, our current mayor, John, "Honey Fitz", Fitzgerald will be our second speaker. The first is the controversial Duncan Troupe of The America Only Party. Can we hear it for our candidates?"

Hope froze, feeling this time like she might pass out.

The well-heeled and educated crowd responded with some fairly enthusiastic as well as polite, tepid applause, with a smattering of cat-calls thrown in.

Nearly everyone in the crowd was well aware of the provocative Troupe and would never attend one of his rallies as it might look like they agreed with his xenophobic views, but were still curious to see him in person to see what the fuss was all about.

As soon as Troupe walked into the room he locked eyes on Hope, as if he had picked her out while spying on the crowd from the kitchen, with an intense look that said,

'I have all the power, don't even think about rejecting my advances. I love beautiful things and you will be mine again. Starting tonight.'

Duncan shook a few hands on his way to the podium after whispering to two burly bodyguards who came over to Hope, one on her right, one her left, opposite bookends that trapped her, preventing any escape on her part.

This is it, this is how it ends for me, I am captured by my past. Duncan Troupe, David van Trap whoever he is will tell everyone about me and my humiliation will be complete. When he finds out about Emily I will lose her to him, too. I lost this game I was playing, it's over.

She was as dejected as she had ever been in her life, and she had experienced her share of life's rough patches.

Well, as it turned out, the game was not over, not quite yet. Someone else had an eagle eye on the whole scene and was waiting, just waiting for that tell-tale sign to pounce.

Dan Billings looked like a rattlesnake coiled and about to attack its prey, a hungry, pissed-off rattlesnake.

Come on, come on, Duncan, boy. Take the bait.

And then, in an instant, everything changed.

As Troupe approached the podium he passed in front of the full-length mirror, stopped, and turned facing it to adjust his tie. He then took two steps away, turned back and faced the mirror again to fix his hair before reaching the lectern, ready to dispense his wisdom to the crowd.

That's it!!! His tell, I knew it!! Billings thoughts screamed.

He had played that move the killer made on the landing of the Doyle's house a thousand times in his head, like a choreographer that patented a dance move and knew it by heart, seeing it on stage in Paris or London, recognizing it as his. Except this unique move executed by Troupe was not diagrammed in pencil on a pad of paper, but documented in cold blood on a hardwood floor.

Dan was now almost positive he found the elusive twenty percent to make the case against Troupe, as long as he got a good prosecutor that could convince a jury of his theory and Monte's evidence held up, that is. It didn't matter, he was going for it.

"Well, folks, it's nice to be among fellow rich people..." Troupe began his folksy-sounding delivery, ready to fire up the crowd, but was rudely interrupted by a non-believer.

Billings screamed, "Now!!!"

The audience, and Duncan, were startled by the outcry. Everyone was confused, with the exception of the policemen attending this event that was turning out to be memorable on so many levels.

Dan rushed to the confused Troupe first and said in a statement that he had prepared in his mind recently many times,

"Duncan Troupe, you are under arrest for the murders of Dennis and Maura Doyle. Cuff him, boys!!!"

Monte reached him next and did the honors, hoping his partner's theory of Troupe's distinctive movements would hold up in court. He roughed Troupe up a little for good measure just in case a well-paid defense attorney was able to get him off, thinking at least he was able to get a couple of licks in for all the hours he and Billings put into the case.

The crowd was stunned, and the festive ballroom that was lively with conversation all evening became unnaturally quiet. Half of the attendees were horrified, never having been exposed to policemen taking a person into custody, especially for murder. The other half just watched in bemused fascination thinking it was just one of Isabella's ideas of putting on some sort of skit for their entertainment.

Troupe, just like Gerry O'Neill was afraid of, may have still got away with the murders with the help of a good lawyer if he had just kept his mouth shut.

"I'll have your badges for this!!! This is an outrage, you stupid

'Mick'!!" Duncan Troupe, leader of The America Only Party and one of Boston's wealthiest citizens sputtered. And, added in front of many credible witnesses,

"It wasn't me!!! Van Trap did it!! It wasn't me!"

What happened next was fascinating, horrifying or inexplicable depending on who was interviewed later. Duncan Troupe began to argue with his alter ego David van Trap, but this time not in private, but for all the world to see.

Shut up, you wimp! Don't say anything, they'll use it against us! It's not too late, just shut the hell up!

"You, shut up, Van Trap! I'm the head of The America Only Party, I have important work to do. You're just a low life murderer. It was you Van Trap that killed that Irish Assistant DA and his wife, not me, Troupe!"

You idiot, I'm you and you're me!

"No, I'm not. You're me and *I'm* you.' There's a difference!"

It's the same thing!

"No, it's not!"

Yes, it is!

People in the audience, especially those from the medical community, realized they were watching a person with a severe psychological disorder in the middle of a breakdown who inexplicably confessed to the gruesome Doyle murders, inadvertently making his case for the prosecution a cakewalk.

The two goons next to Hope knew their employment would no longer be needed and hastily headed for the exits.

Van Trap/Troupe just continued to babble on saying, "He drowned Taffy, too," referring to the Troupe family's beloved Husky-German Shepard mix that was found floating in the family pool so many years ago.

"Who the hell is Taffy?" Monte asked, letting Troupe run his mouth off some more before hauling him off.

Duncan Troupe just kept talking and talking in front of all those believable witnesses. When the detectives knew he confessed enough to cook his own goose, Monte pushed him along toward the elevators and a free ride to the stationhouse, but not before reaching into his pocket and forking over a fresh five-dollar bill to Dan.

The crowd was no longer silent, now murmuring and most in a state of total disbelief except for a few worldly ones such as the current mayor of Boston, "Honey Fitz", that had a bemused look on his face as he waited for his turn to speak.

Isabella, another person who was never surprised by what her fellow man is capable of and not at all thrown off by the debacle, strode to the podium once again.

"Well, I did promise you an interesting evening, one you could tell your friends about tomorrow morning! Our next speaker…"

Victor made his way back to Hope while Fitzgerald spoke, his date looking like she had just given birth, totally exhausted, yet relieved, joyful.

"Are you alright, Hope? All this excitement too much for you? Quite a night, don't you agree?"

Hope Davis just looked in his eyes and said, now able to let her defenses down, maybe for the first time in her life,

"I suppose that's an excellent observation, Dr. Victor Siegel. But I wouldn't expect anything less from the next Chief of Surgery at Massachusetts General Hospital," cracking a wry smile.

Epilogue

The papers ran the story of Isabella's fundraiser at the Parker House Hotel for weeks, inadvertently generating publicity for Mass General, which made its fundraising campaign wildly successful. People gobbled up anything they could read about the Doyle murders and Troupe, becoming familiar with such psychological terms as 'split personality' and 'narcissistic disorder' and the fine distinction between 'sociopath' and 'psychopath'. When there was nothing left factually to write about, newspapers ran offbeat pseudo-scientific articles such as *Is the Increase of Electricity Use in the Home Leading to More Cases of Mental Illness?* Eventually the public had their fill and the story began to fade from the public's eye.

Victor did get the position at Mass General, interestingly, by unanimous vote. His workload has increased dramatically, but he still manages to play hockey most Thursday nights, now traveling in a stylish Packard after being convinced to retire his ramshackle 'Tin Lizzy'.

Hope received her degree, Cum Laude, from Simmons College and procured a position as an assistant librarian at Boston Public Library. She is currently taking classes in the Jewish faith with an eye toward becoming Mrs. Victor Siegel next June.

Hope and Victor's table won the 'opposites' contest, allowing them to experience another memorable evening in the presence of Isabella Stuart Gardner, this one purely enjoyable. Isabella's distinctive home inspired them to consider Venice as a possible honeymoon destination.

Colleen went back to work in the ER and would eventually become head nurse, remaining at her beloved Mass General the rest of her career. Billings and Gallo must have rubbed off on Mike who got his detective's shield with the Cambridge Police Department on his first try. The Flynn's remained close friends of Hope and Victor for the rest of their lives, Hope keeping up her end of the bargain by never telling Tommy she was his birthmother. Mike and Colleen had the means to move from Dana Street to a single family home but always found reasons not to, their ties to the building just too strong. "Maybe next year."

Tommy continued to excel at baseball, but remained very shy and withdrawn due to his scratchy voice, especially around girls. That would change when a new family moved into the third floor of Dana Street, the late father having been one of Mary Vilkas' favorite co-workers at the thriving shoe factory in Jamaica Plain where they were employed for years. The family had a daughter Tommy's age, Kelly Burke, who he fell head over heels in love with at first sight, beginning yet another chapter in his life. Tommy would chase after her for years until she decided the time was right, and caught him.

Ignas and Mary Vilkas added Alphonse and Leo to their brood, hoping their new sons would emulate Peter instead of the high-spirited, always skirting trouble, Eddy. Eventually maturing and finally able to sit still, Eddy became an excellent student and directed his considerable energy into a successful career as an electrical engineer, designing some of the country's largest power plants.

Sister Apollonia shared her unique talent with the city of Boston as guest violinist with the Boston Symphony Orchestra, and brought the house down. She even composed her own symphony, meticulously written in pen and ink on parchment, which has yet to be performed.

Gerry O'Neil's life was back on track, and his name was floated about town to be the new dean of Suffolk University School of Law. He still manages to play Wollaston with the boys as often as possible and managed to get his handicap down to single digits.

Monte started to incorporate photography to identify the unique markings made by gun barrels on a bullet as an added tool in his expanding forensic arsenal. After a few days of basking in the glow of cracking the Doyle case, Captain Moore rewarded him and Dan with a very complex, diabolical murder to solve, which, naturally, he greeted with a predictable, resounding string of expletives. Monte was trying to break his habit of swearing so often, but, "With the work we do it's fucking hard, you know."

Ellen was introduced to a shy doctor at Mass General and they are currently dating, taking it very slowly, but both parties seem happy. She recently added bridal magazines to the stack on her coffee table.

Penelope Hinckley was offered the job of Director of Admissions for Simmons College which she graciously accepted. She and Hope remained close, often attending The Boston Symphony together. The two women had a lot to talk about after the evening Sister Apollonia performed, Hope's filling in her friend about her caper at The Mary Magdalen Adoption Agency, which seemed a lifetime ago.

Pottle and Lockhart became alarmed when they realized their candidate from The America Only Party had a legitimate chance to win as Boston Mayor and quit the business. They pooled their resources and bought a coffee shop on Beacon Hill, which became a favored hangout for State House political hacks and other persons with a lot of time on their hands.

Billings was not quite done with Duncan Troupe, the man that constantly mocked his Irish heritage every chance he got, even after he was firmly secured in prison.

This is for you, Gram and Pap, Dan's beloved grandparents that barely survived the Irish Potato Famine only to be spit on when they arrived in Boston. Billings shared a trait of many of his Irish brethren, that of having long memories, and payback is a bitch.

Dan arranged for Mr. Troupe to have an Irish prosecutor, an Irish Judge, Irish guards and when he was found guilty and sentenced to prison before his date with "Old Sparky", the affectionate term for Massachusetts' electric chair, an Irish "roommate". His name was Mike McGuirk, considered the meanest, most violent and most feared inmate in the system.

By the time McGuirk gets through with them, both Troupe and Van Trap will be begging for the chair, Dan laughed to himself.

Fredrick Troupe lived long enough to see his only son vilified in the public eye and became withdrawn and depressed. He left this world gasping for breath when his nurse inadvertently parked his wheelchair on his oxygen hose, the undertakers using every trick they knew to get his contorted body to be suitable for viewing for the few that bothered to show up. He died extremely wealthy, but a totally broken man.

Fredrick and Duncan Troupe's estates were eventually put in the hands of the probate court and word filtered down to the policemen that worked security for The America Only Party to send in a claim for their time, including the event at the Parker House Hotel. They were pleasantly surprised to not only get reimbursed, but a generous termination bonus thrown in as well.

Dan used this windfall to buy his car.

The court also used some of the Troupe's fortune to commission a lasting monument, not for anything to do with the Troupe family name, but ironically for the survivors of the Irish Potato Famine that came to Boston. Such a memorial can be found in Boston on School Street, a few blocks away from the site of the Parker House Hotel.

So, who is Tommy's birthfather? Have you read *The Shoemaker's Castle?*

CPSIA information can be obtained
at www.ICGtesting.com
Printed in the USA
BVOW09s0035110817

491581BV00001B/103/P